MISS PICKERELL AND
THE LOST WORLD

MISS PICKERELL AND THE LOST WORLD

by Dora Pantell

Julius Schwartz,
Science Consultant

Series originated by
Ellen MacGregor
Illustrated by Charles Geer

Franklin Watts
New York/London/Toronto/Sydney
1986

Library of Congress Cataloging-in-Publication Data

Pantell, Dora F.
    Miss Pickerell and the lost world.

    "Series originated by Ellen MacGregor."
    Summary: When a flood in Square Toe County washes
in a strange creature, Miss Pickerell goes on a
perilous journey to return it to its native habitat.
    [1. Wildlife conservation—Fiction.   2. Mice—
Fiction]   I. Geer, Charles, ill.   II. Title.
PZ7.P1934Mh   1986   [Fic]   86-13353
ISBN 0-531-10229-7

CONTENTS

For beautiful Maritza, whose triumphs on the typewriter are matched only by her exquisite patience and unfailing understanding.

MISS PICKERELL AND THE LOST WORLD

1

A FLOOD
IN SQUARE
TOE COUNTY

Miss Pickerell clapped her two hands firmly over her ears, shook her head from side to side so that her eyeglasses slipped still another inch farther down on her nose, and, to make absolutely sure, shut her eyes tight. If only for an instant, she wanted to forget the sight of her seven nieces and nephews and to stop hearing the sound of their screeching in her peaceful farmhouse kitchen. The constant blaring of the radio that Dwight, her oldest nephew, carried with him wherever he went was even worse than the screeching. Miss Pickerell sighed heavily. She also uttered a small hopeful sigh when she half opened one eye and saw that all seven children were getting ready to race out of the house.

"I just don't know," she commented, as she tucked a loose hairpin into place and turned to

Pumpkins, her big black cat, who was snoozing on a sunny windowsill, "I just don't know how their mother can expect me to keep them here until Friday. Today's only Saturday and they've given me a splitting headache already."

Pumpkins twitched his tail to show that he had heard. He made no other reply. Miss Pickerell did not find it in her heart to blame him. This was the first day in more than a week that it had not rained. And she knew how much Pumpkins loved a good nap in the sunshine.

"Those children all talk at once," she went on. "That's what makes them so difficult."

Sampson, the small dog with the freckled ears who now made his home on the mountaintop farm, barked briefly. Miss Pickerell was not entirely sure whether this was his answer to her or one more statement about how annoyed he was. No matter how many times he tried, he simply could not manage to jump up as high as the windowsill.

"But even when they talk one at a time," Miss Pickerell continued, still thinking out loud, "they are a problem, always up to SOMETHING. Euphus with his curiosity about science is the worst of all. And when he talks . . ."

Miss Pickerell adored her middle nephew, Euphus. She felt extremely proud of him as well. He was very smart in school, especially in science. But when he sometimes explained a science idea to her, he talked so fast and used such long words that she hardly understood him. Some of the words she could not even find when she looked them up in her encyclopedia.

"He says that's because science is moving so fast and the encyclopedia hasn't caught up with it yet," Miss Pickerell added indignantly. "Not even the brand-new set that I bought from that nice young door-to-door salesman last year. Or was it the year before?"

Pumpkins made no comment. Sampson barked again, much louder this time. Miss Pickerell gave him a sympathetic glance. She could never forget how lonely and unhappy he was when she found him abandoned on the road. She wanted to do anything she could to make things up to him.

"All right! All right!" she said. "I'll lift you up."

Pumpkins politely moved over to make room for his friend. He also proceeded to give the dog a good face wash. Miss Pickerell patted Sampson's head and decided that, in her opinion, animals were far more sensible than children, and looked out at her back lawn and kitchen garden. The heavy spring rains had melted most of the snow from the trees and the bushes. Soon the cold would be gone and it would be time for planting again. Miss Pickerell smiled as she made a mental note of which flowers and vegetables she would plant. She had just finished the list of the flowers and was starting on the vegetables when the ringing of the telephone brought her sharply back to the present.

"It's probably their mother calling to ask about

the children," she told herself as she walked across the kitchen to where the telephone hung on the wall next to her shiny black coal stove. "Or maybe even their father who's such a worrier. I won't say anything to him, but I'm a little concerned myself now. Where could they all have run off to so suddenly?"

But it was not the children's father on the telephone. It was the high nasal voice of Miss Lemon, Square Toe City's chief telephone operator, that Miss Pickerell heard when she picked up the receiver. She groaned silently. Miss Lemon was a long talker. And since she listened in on so many telephone conversations, she always had a lot to talk about.

"Good morning, Miss Pickerell," she began now. "A lovely day it's turning out to be, isn't it?"

"Very," Miss Pickerell agreed politely.

"The switchboard is quiet at the moment," Miss Lemon went on. "And I did want to give you the very latest news."

Miss Pickerell reached out for the stool with the oilcloth-covered cushion on it and sat down. She wondered, as Miss Lemon drew in the long deep breath that always preceded any relaying of information, why telephone calls in Square Toe City were still connected over a switchboard. Practically everything else was fully automated and computerized.

"What news, Miss Lemon?" she prompted now, hoping that the operator would get to the point, and counting, at the same time, the ten chimes that her new kitchen clock was ringing out. "What latest news did you want to give me?"

"Oh, before I go into that," Miss Lemon laughed, her voice gaily gliding up and down the scale, "I really must tell you that somebody who shall remain NAMELESS, of course, saw Dwight, your oldest nephew, taking your four youngest nieces and nephews in to see the early Saturday morning picture show."

"NAMELESS indeed!" Miss Pickerell snorted. "I can tell you exactly who that SOMEBODY was. Her name begins with a . . ."

"But I must keep my little secret, mustn't I?" Miss Lemon interrupted, laughing again. "I must also say that I agree with this person. It is hardly the kind of picture young children should be seeing. All full of blood and violence, I understand."

"What movies aren't these days?" Miss Pickerell sighed.

Miss Lemon exhaled a very loud breath as she sighed with Miss Pickerell. She inhaled another before returning to her conversation.

"Are those children going to spend their entire spring vacation with you, Miss Pickerell?" she asked.

"Certainly not!" Miss Pickerell replied instantly, not even bothering to ask how Miss Lemon already knew that their mother had left them with her only yesterday. "Just until their parents return from Plentibush City. Their father wanted to visit Mr. Esticott, our retired train conductor, who is now living there with his daughter."

"I'm aware of that," Miss Lemon said.

Miss Pickerell did not doubt it for a moment.

"And their mother," Miss Pickerell continued, "wanted to be out of the house during the time it would take the painter to replaster the ceiling in the entrance hall and for the paperhanger to paste her new flowered grass cloth up on the parlor walls."

"I don't approve of that at all," Miss Lemon went on to say bluntly. "When she comes back, she may well find that the ceiling hasn't been completely plastered and that the grass-cloth wallpaper is crooked in a number of places."

Miss Pickerell couldn't agree more. But she preferred not to discuss it.

"I believe you said that you had some news for me, Miss Lemon," she said, changing the subject.

"Two pieces of news, actually," Miss Lemon replied. "The first is about our flood early this morning."

"Flood?" Miss Pickerell echoed. "Did you say FLOOD, Miss Lemon?"

Miss Lemon let out another sigh, this one of deep disappointment.

"I keep forgetting," she said, "that you people up in the mountains don't always know about what's happening down in the valley. But I must admit that I find it hard to believe that, even up on your mountain farm, you didn't hear that our Square Toe River overflowed."

Miss Pickerell's heart skipped a beat. She had

visions of houses floating in the streets and of people and animals fleeing desperately up the hills for safety. And her seven nieces and nephews? Dwight and the younger children were at the movies. But WHERE were Euphus and Rosemary?

"Was . . . was it very bad?" she asked anxiously.

"Bad enough," Miss Lemon replied. "No wonder, with all that rain from the mountains gushing down without a stop into the river. I have heard that the river was simply CHOKING and HAD to overflow its banks."

"Yes, yes, I understand," Miss Pickerell said. "But the people, the people living in the houses near the river and . . . ?"

"Oh, the Governor spoke to them," Miss Lemon replied calmly, "the very minute that he heard about the swollen river and the way it was flooding the luncheonette and the barbershop in what he called the disaster area. He spoke on television and advised everybody to abandon all shops and houses and to run as fast and as far away as they could."

This time, Miss Pickerell felt her heart sink way down into her shoes.

"Have they all managed to escape?" she asked. "Are they safe?"

"Well, they must be," Miss Lemon said. "The Mayor went on television after the Governor did, and he told everybody to come right back. Didn't you hear his speech, either, Miss Pickerell?"

"I . . . I don't watch much television," Miss Pickerell said weakly.

"I suppose I can understand that," Miss Lemon replied. "In a *way* I can, that is. But, as I often say, there's a great deal we miss when we don't watch. There is, for example, that show about . . ."

Miss Lemon sounded as though she had settled in for a good long talk. Miss Pickerell did not like to hurt Miss Lemon's feelings, but her patience was beginning to wear thin.

"Miss Lemon," she broke in the minute she heard the operator pause for a breath between sentences. "Did you want to tell me about the second piece of news you mentioned?"

"Gladly," Miss Lemon replied immediately. "It's about the unknown world."

"*The unknown world!*" Miss Pickerell exclaimed.

"The unknown world," Miss Lemon repeated. "That's what Professor Humwhistel called it when he spoke to the Governor a few minutes ago. He was telling the Governor about the trunk of a freshly cut pine tree that had been washed up on the overflowing river. And on the branch of that tree, Miss Pickerell, on that branch, there was an ANIMAL from the unknown world. Can you believe that, Miss Pickerell?"

Miss Pickerell nearly said "Pooh!" She would definitely have said it, if one of her seven nieces and nephews had told her about such a creature. But this was Professor Humwhistel, a distinguished man of science who never, absolutely never, made up wild stories. On the other hand, he was sometimes very absentminded and perhaps he . . .

Miss Pickerell was still mulling this over in her mind when Miss Lemon asked whether she would be driving down to the valley to see things for herself. Miss Pickerell did not think so. There was a lot she had to do this morning. To begin with, she was going to take Nancy Agatha, her cow, up to the pasture.

"Poor Nancy Agatha!" she explained to Miss Lemon. "She's been shut up in her barn all week. But she'd have caught her death of cold if I'd let her out in that terrible weather. Thank you for calling, Miss Lemon, and for giving me the news."

"Not at all," Miss Lemon said sweetly. "I'll call again later. To give you the news about Euphus and about your oldest niece, Rosemary."

"EUPHUS AND ROSEMARY?" Miss Pickerell nearly screamed into the mouthpiece. "What has happened to them?"

Her teeth were beginning to chatter. Her knees felt so weak she was afraid she might fall off the stool. And Miss Lemon was taking her time about answering.

"Nothing that I know of *so far*," she said at last. "But I can tell you, Miss Pickerell, that Mrs. Broadribb, your neighbor, called her best friend, Mr. Trilling, our Square Toe City piano tuner, to say that she saw them run off with Professor Humwhistel. And Professor Humwhistel had that strange animal from an unknown world in his hands."

Miss Pickerell took a large white handkerchief out of her pocket and wiped the cool beads of perspiration from her face. She wished she could tell Miss Lemon exactly what she thought of her for frightening her nearly out of her wits. But Miss Lemon had gone off the line. And Miss Pickerell had no intention whatsoever of calling her back.

2
AN ARRIVAL FROM AN UNKNOWN WORLD

Nancy Agatha mooed gratefully when Miss Pickerell led her out of the barn. And when they walked to the pasture together, Miss Pickerell felt that her cow would have jumped up and down with joy if only she had been able to. As Miss Lemon had announced, it was turning out to be a beautiful day. The warm sun glowed on the mountaintops and in the valleys that lay serenely between them. Spring was definitely on the way in. Miss Pickerell thought she could almost hear the stirring of the daisies and the dandelions as they struggled to push their way out of the ground.

"This is no day to spend cleaning up my closets," she said, half to herself and half to Nancy Agatha. "A ride in the automobile will be much nicer. It will help settle my nerves. And you and

Pumpkins and Sampson will love the ride, won't you?"

Miss Pickerell always took her animals with her when she went out for a ride. Nancy Agatha stood in the little red trailer that was attached to the automobile. The trailer had an embroidered canvas awning over it to protect the cow from bad weather. Pumpkins and Sampson sometimes sat in the trailer with Nancy Agatha. Most of the time, though, they sat in front with Miss Pickerell, Pumpkins on her lap and Sampson on the seat next to her.

"I'll go nowhere near the river and those poor places that nearly floated away," Miss Pickerell promised herself as she settled the animals for the ride. She then ran into the house to get the knitting bag that she used as a purse and the big black umbrella that she always liked to take along. At the last minute she decided to put on her new mauve jacket and the black felt hat that she jabbed into place with a hatpin. After all, she reflected, spring was *not really* here, much as she would have liked to think so.

She thought about this again when she began steering her car down the private road that led to the highway. The rain was gone but it had left the mud. She kept sloshing around in it. Once she very nearly got stuck and thought seriously about turning back. She changed her mind when she neared the end of the road and could see the highway ahead.

But the highway presented its own difficulties. Miss Pickerell—who practically never drove her automobile more than thirty miles an hour—made sure to drive in the right-hand lane, so as not to slow the other drivers. Today, however, all of them seemed to be in an extra-special hurry. They kept honking and shouting for her to get out of the way. One driver even gave her a long angry blast of his horn after he passed her. Miss Pickerell did not pay him much mind.

"It will be better once we get to Square Toe City," she reassured Sampson, who had barked back at every honk. "We're very nearly there."

At the intersection leading into Square Toe City, Miss Pickerell turned left so that she could drive along the streets she liked best. She particularly enjoyed Mulberry Avenue, with its big, old elm trees, its tidy, white-painted houses, and the small, old-fashioned shops alongside some of the houses. She waved to the shoemaker, who was sitting outside his shop and had said, "Good morning, Miss Pickerell" the minute he saw her.

"I'll stop by to see him some other time," Miss Pickerell decided as she quickly drove past the store. "He'll probably want to talk about the flood today. I'll go see Mr. Kettelson, instead. He talks only about how bad the hardware store business is. That's not so upsetting as listening to talk about the flood."

Miss Pickerell cut short her ride on Mulberry Avenue and steered in the direction of Main Street. Things were always changing there, she knew. But she gasped when she saw how many more changes had taken place since her last visit, a month ago. The trolley barn, which housed a library after buses came to take the place of the bright yellow street-cars, was now a pickle factory. The bakery, where the doors always stood open and the delicious smells of the freshly baked bread greeted everyone who passed, was now a bank. Machines for depositing and taking out money were built into its walls. Miss Pickerell shuddered. She would never dream of doing any banking business with a machine. She shuddered again when she saw that the drugstore with the lovely blue and green jars in the window had disappeared. A billboard announced that a tall co-op apartment building would soon be going up in its place.

Only Mr. Kettelson's hardware store seemed unchanged. The same shiny display of pots and pans stood in the first row of the window. Directly behind them were the toasters, the broilers, and the brooms and the brushes, their bristles neatly covered with plastic. Cans of paint, containers of wax, and bottles of furniture polish were in the rear of the store, next to the gardening shovels and an air conditioner with the sign SPECIAL BUY pasted across it. Miss Pickerell couldn't imagine anyone in breezy Square Toe City wanting to buy an air conditioner. She planned to speak to Mr. Kettelson about this example of poor business judgment on his part. But Mr. Kettelson spoke first. He ran out of the shop to greet her the instant he caught sight of the trailer.

"I'm so happy to see you, Miss Pickerell," he said. "You are well, I hope? And Nancy Agatha, too? And Pumpkins and Sampson, of course? Please come in."

"Thank you," Miss Pickerell replied, accepting both the invitation and the metal folding-chair that Mr. Kettelson set up for her near his front window. "I'll be able to keep an eye on the animals from here," she said.

Mr. Kettelson nodded and pulled up a chair for himself. He looked even sadder and more nervous than usual, Miss Pickerell observed. His long, thin face had no color in it at all. And the few gray hairs that he had on his head stuck out every which way.

"How have you been feeling, Mr. Kettelson?" she asked, a little anxiously.

"As well as can be expected, Miss Pickerell," he answered, "under the circumstances."

"Oh?" she asked, waiting for him to continue.

"It was those stacks of burlap bags!" he exclaimed almost immediately. "Those heavy bags that I dragged down to the river so that they could be filled with sand and placed on the riverbank. They would help to hold back the flood, I thought."

"That was very clever of you," Miss Pickerell offered.

"They didn't do much good, I'm afraid," Mr. Kettelson sighed. "And I still feel the cramps in my arms."

"Liniment," Miss Pickerell recommended instantly. "Liniment rubbed in briskly after a good hot bath to ease the . . ."

"But that wasn't the worst part," Mr. Kettelson broke in. He then sprang out of his chair and started pacing between the shelves that contained his paint buckets and brushes and those that displayed light bulbs of various shapes and sizes. "The worst part was what they did to that poor animal, the one who floated in on the tree trunk."

Miss Pickerell opened her mouth without saying anything. She swallowed twice.

"It was all those reporters who kept popping flashbulbs into the creature's eyes," Mr. Kettelson continued, now talking almost as fast as he was pacing. "They had all arrived because of the flood. The animal on the tree trunk seemed to them even more important, though. They kept scribbling in their books and taking more and more pictures, from the front, from the sides, from every angle. Nobody cared that the poor thing was so wet and looked so frightened."

"But . . . but Professor Humwhistel . . . ," Miss Pickerell breathed.

"Yes," Mr. Kettelson said. "The animal being a small one, Professor Humwhistel was able to grab it and to start running away. But with the newspaper and television people at his *heels*, Miss Pickerell. You see, Professor Humwhistel, who was helping to fill the sandbags and who saw the creature float in, remarked that it was a very *strange animal*, one he had never seen on earth. He even commented that it might be from *another world.*"

"Oh?" Miss Pickerell whispered.

"And the television people kept shouting that they wanted to pose the first animal from another world on a television TALK SHOW," Mr. Kettelson continued. "They said that the public was entitled to that. Your middle nephew, Euphus, and your oldest niece, Rosemary, were very good at running in front of the TV people and blocking their way. Professor Humwhistel was finally able to lock himself up in his office with the two of them and the animal."

"And that's where they are now?" Miss Pickerell asked quickly.

"Not according to Miss Lemon," Mr. Kettelson replied. "She says that Professor Humwhistel called the Mayor to say he was leaving by a side door to take the animal to Mr. Blakely's office."

Miss Pickerell sat bolt upright. She had NO confidence whatsoever in Mr. Blakely's feeling for animals.

"What does HE have to do with it?" she asked, as fast as she could get the words out of her mouth.

"He's been promoted," Mr. Kettelson, who shared her fears about Mr. Blakely, sighed. "He is no longer Deputy Administrator in charge of directing space-flight traffic. His official title is now Deputy Administrator in charge of checking on all objects, radiations, and evidences of life coming to this planet from outer space. He will stop at nothing to learn the reasons for this latest arrival. I wouldn't put it past him to try some kind of animal lie-detector test to . . ."

"But this animal is NOT from outer space," Miss Pickerell interrupted, dismissing the idea of the lie-detector test as out of the question and concentrating on what was important. "Professor Humwhistel said it was from an unknown world."

"He also said that it was from a LOST world," Mr. Kettelson corrected. "Miss Lemon may not have overheard everything. But no one knows exactly where that lost world exists."

"Forevermore!" Miss Pickerell whispered.

"And, of course," Mr. Kettelson added glumly, "no one knows exactly how kind the Deputy Administrator will be to a strange animal from a lost world, either. If that turns out to be true, we don't even know what he plans to do with the animal or . . ."

"I, for one, soon will," Miss Pickerell declared, getting out of her metal folding-chair and heading for the door. "I'm going to have a good long talk with Deputy Administrator Blakely about his intentions."

"I'm going with you," Mr. Kettelson said. "You'll need me to stay outside with Pumpkins and Sampson and Nancy Agatha while you're in his office."

He pulled the shutters down over his shop window and double-locked the door. He checked the

lock six or seven times before he joined Miss Pickerell in the automobile.

"I don't really believe anybody will want to
steal that air conditioner," he said, smiling a little.
"But your neighbor, Mrs. Broadribb, who came into
the shop to buy a frying pan this morning, believes
that this animal is only a beginning, that there will
be other strange animals from outer space, some
who will even steal everything they can lay their
hands on."

Miss Pickerell did not take the time to reply.
She was too busy thinking about what Deputy Administrator Blakely might say to her and about what
she would most definitely say to him. She released
her brakes, considered for a moment the idea of
making a quick U-turn in the middle of the street,
decided against committing such an unlawful act,
and, watching her speedometer climb steadily up to
thirty-five miles per hour, drove straight ahead.

3
A MOST UNUSUAL ANIMAL

Miss Pickerell had never liked Deputy Administrator Blakely's office. She had no objections to the charts and maps and the space capsule mock-ups that practically lined the walls. On the contrary, she wholly approved of them as an important part of his work. She did not even object too strongly to the bulging briefcase that he kept locking and unlocking impatiently whenever she was in the office. But she never felt really comfortable in his extremely high straight-backed chairs. And she simply could not understand the three pictures that hung over his desk. Their lines and circles did not look like anything she believed really belonged in a picture. The largest picture, the one with the bright yellow dot in the middle of a lot of white paint, she found particularly exasperating. Most of all, though, she disliked Miss Dudley, the lady with the steel-blue eyes and the blonde corkscrew curls who sat in the room outside the Deputy Administrator's office. Miss Dudley never gave up trying to keep her from going in to see Mr. Blakely.

But it was not Miss Dudley who was guarding the door today. It was Mr. Trilling, Square Toe City's piano tuner, sitting in her chair and looking just as watchful. Miss Pickerell could not hide her surprise.

"I understand," Mr. Trilling said mournfully, after listening to Miss Pickerell's second *oh* of disbelief. "Mrs. Broadribb was quite certain that you would find it a little odd when you found out."

Miss Pickerell uttered another almost soundless *oh*.

"You see," Mr. Trilling went on, "the piano-tuning business has been unusually poor lately, and when Miss Dudley left and the job became vacant, I offered my services to Mr. Blakely. I advised the Deputy Administrator very frankly that I didn't know how to type. Still, I felt I could easily learn. After all, hitting the keys on a typewriter shouldn't be totally different from working with them on a piano."

Miss Pickerell refrained from saying anything about this. She kept gazing steadily at the door to the inner office and wondering about the best way to get through it. Mr. Trilling understood.

"I'm afraid that's completely impossible," he said curtly. "The Deputy Administrator is confer-

ring with the Governor and the Mayor and a number of other very important people."

"Humph!" Miss Pickerell retorted. "I probably know every one of those people, and you know
that, too."

"It's a very secret conference," Mr. Trilling
said stiffly.

"I also happen to know," Miss Pickerell replied
with equal stiffness, "EXACTLY what they're con-
ferring about."

"Then you have heard about that . . . that animal?" Mr. Trilling asked, whispering.

"Certainly," Miss Pickerell told him. "I have
an idea that all of Square Toe County has heard
about it by now."

"Miss Lemon?" Mr. Trilling asked, still whispering.

"Miss Lemon," Miss Pickerell replied, whispering back.

She felt tempted to tell him that Miss Lemon
had also reported on his conversation with Mrs.
Broadribb about Dwight and the Saturday morning
picture show. But she didn't want to waste any
more time.

"Mr. Trilling," she said, standing up very
straight so that she could more easily look right into
his eyes, "I respect your desire to obey the Deputy
Administrator's orders. But I have a most important
reason for wanting to see him. *And* if you don't let
me in through that door, I'll find another way."

"That's exactly what Miss Ogelthorpe said when she wanted to go in," Mr. Trilling cried out.

"Miss Ogelthorpe, the lady reporter from the *Square Toe Gazette*?" Miss Pickerell inquired.

Mr. Trilling nodded sadly.

"She said that she had outrun all the other reporters," he added, "and that she wasn't going to give up after that. I . . . I had to let her in."

Miss Pickerell fixed her gaze on him again.

"And now?" she asked.

Mr. Trilling threw his hands out in a gesture of despair. "Well," he said, between what seemed to be absolutely clenched teeth, "only if you go in very quietly. And IF you sit in the back."

Miss Pickerell saw no chair in the back for her to sit on when she tiptoed into the office. Every chair had been drawn up around Mr. Blakely's long and very low conference table in the middle of the room.

Deputy Administrator Blakely, stony-faced and erect, was sitting on the far side of the table. The Governor was on his right-hand side, and the Mayor on his left. As always, the Governor's bow tie was carefully knotted, and the ends of his brown moustache very neatly waxed. The Mayor, his jacket flung over the back of his chair, was in his usual shirt-sleeves. It was a light green shirt today, Miss Pickerell noted, with white polka dots. Professor Humwhistel, sitting between the Mayor and Dr. Haggerty, Miss Pickerell's beloved veterinarian, seemed to be concentrating only on how far down he could slump in his chair. Euphus and Rosemary were on the opposite side of the table, next to Miss Ogelthorpe, who was standing up for a moment to smooth down her skirt. Miss Pickerell observed that the skirt had orange and purple flowers on it and that Miss Ogelthorpe had on very high heels. How she was able to outrun the other reporters, Miss Pickerell could not imagine.

It was the Mayor who saw Miss Pickerell first. He gave her a broad, cheery smile.

"Come, Miss Pickerell," he called out. "Come and look at this strange creature we have on the Deputy Administrator's table. Miss Ogelthorpe was kind enough to wrap the shivering animal in her scarf. But you can easily push that aside and . . ."

The Deputy Administrator raised his eyebrows and threw the Mayor an icy look. The Mayor stopped talking. He got up from the table to give Miss Pickerell his seat.

"We are very puzzled," the Governor commented. "I may even say *extremely* puzzled about this animal, Miss Pickerell."

"We have none of us seen anything exactly like it," Deputy Administrator Blakely added. "And we none of us agree on where it might have come from. My own opinion is that it descended from outer space."

Miss Pickerell looked from Professor Humwhistel to Dr. Haggerty and back again to Professor Humwhistel. She valued their opinions most of all. Neither of them said a word. The Mayor remarked that he did not believe she needed to be afraid to touch the animal. Rosemary shouted across the table that her Aunt Lavinia wasn't afraid of any animal.

"Nor of anything else, evidently," the Deputy Administrator commented dryly. "Or she wouldn't keep getting herself mixed up in one dangerous adventure after another. And getting me involved in some of them, too."

"If you are referring to the time I asked you to get me a ticket on the space shuttle to the moon, Mr. Deputy Administrator," Miss Pickerell retorted heatedly, "I can say only that . . ."

"I have asked you a thousand times," Mr. Blakely interrupted, "not to call me Mr. Deputy Administrator. I have suggested that you address me as Mr. Blakely. I have . . ."

"Please!" the Governor boomed, banging on the table with a hard-covered, oversized appointment book that he had hastily picked up from the Deputy Administrator's desk. "We must get on with this unpleasant business."

"Yes, Governor," Miss Pickerell said. "I will go ahead now."

"At any rate," the Mayor laughed, "I believe that we can assure Deputy Administrator Blakely that Miss Pickerell is not getting into any dangerous adventure now."

"One never knows," Professor Humwhistel said, heaving a sigh that nearly blew away three

36

sheets of yellow paper on the table before him. "With Miss Pickerell, one NEVER knows."

Miss Pickerell did not answer. She was busy polishing her glasses. She inspected them twice to make sure that they were clean. Then she strained forward to lean over the newspaper spread across the table to look at the unknown creature wrapped in the scarf. She could hear how the Mayor, standing in back of her, was holding his breath, and she could practically feel the hard stare of the Governor fixed on the back of her neck. She reached over, carefully moved aside the colored scarf, took a very long look, and stood up suddenly. She was laughing uncontrollably. Her whole body shook with her helpless laughter.

"She's hysterical!" the Governor shouted. "Someone should slap her. A quick sharp slap, my wife always says. Or perhaps some smelling salts . . ."

"No! No!" Miss Pickerell gasped, beginning at last to get a hold on herself. "I'm perfectly all right. I was just so . . . so astonished by what I saw."

"What DID you see?" Miss Ogelthorpe, wildly waving her pad and pencil, screamed across the room.

"What IS it?" the Governor boomed. "Tell us IMMEDIATELY what this strange animal is!"

"A . . . a mouse," Miss Pickerell said, starting to laugh all over again. "Nothing but a mouse. A very pretty and a *most* unusual one, I admit, but . . ."

Her laughter came to a sudden stop when she saw the Deputy Administrator uncoil himself from his chair, then give her a very stern stare.

"It is NOT a mouse," he declared.

The sound of his voice was so sharp and penetrating that the animal on the table trembled violently enough for the newspaper to crackle under it. And Mr. Trilling even opened the door cautiously to see if something terrible was happening inside.

Mr. Blakely looked up at him and said, "I'm sorry."

Miss Pickerell whispered, "Forevermore!"

4
EUPHUS EXPLAINS ABOUT SQUIRRELS AND KANGAROOS

"I'm sorry," Mr. Blakely said again, as he slowly lowered himself back into his chair. "But this animal bears no resemblance to any mouse I have ever seen. Not on earth, at any rate. Perhaps in outer space, where you . . ."

He looked pointedly at Miss Pickerell. She shook her head. What a ridiculous idea! Of course she had seen no mice on Mars or the moon when she had been there. And she had no intention of going back to see if she could find any. She was definitely not getting mixed up in what the Deputy Administrator called her "dangerous adventures." Not in outer space or anywhere else!!

"You seem very thoughtful, Miss Pickerell," Mr. Blakely, who was still staring at her, remarked. "Perhaps you will tell us what's on your mind."

Miss Pickerell shook her head, more vigorously

this time. Another thing she did not intend to do was to tell the Deputy Administrator about the uneasy feeling she had that there might be something in what he was saying. The poor animal, wrapped again in Miss Ogelthorpe's orange and purple scarf, was unlike any mouse *she* had ever seen, either. The fur was still wet and badly matted but, she had observed, it was distinctly brown, rather than the usual mouse-gray. The very furry tail had a number of broad, black stripes on it. The eyes, filled with fear when they looked up at her, were uncommonly large. The ears were still more strange. They were soft and fluffy and so long that they drooped, with the ends actually folded under the animal's chin. And the feet were white! Miss Pickerell rubbed her two forefingers across her forehead and turned to Dr. Haggerty. She gave him an urgently inquiring look. He smiled his usual small smile, ran his fingers through his sandy-colored hair, and sat up a little straighter.

"It *is* a mouse," he said quietly. "Definitely a mouse, Miss Pickerell."

Professor Humwhistel, now fumbling with the heavy watch chain that dangled across his tightly buttoned-up vest, stood up and cleared his throat.

"What do you think, Professor?" Miss Pickerell asked instantly.

The Professor did not answer for a moment. He stooped over the table to squint through his gold-rimmed spectacles first.

"I have only the highest respect for the expert opinion of our young and able veterinarian," he said. "But I must confess that I remain a little bewildered."

"*Bewildered!*" Deputy Administrator Blakely shouted. "I should think so!"

Professor Humwhistel smiled.

"The poor thing's asleep, I believe," he said, in an aside to Dr. Haggerty.

"Fatigue," Dr. Haggerty replied. "No wonder, after being submerged in the cold river water. Fatigue and some shock, too, I suspect."

"Please go on, Professor," the Governor insisted. "I have a number of important matters waiting for me at the State Capital. If I am to keep this proud State of ours on the map, I must, as always, attend to its business."

Professor Humwhistel said that he understood.

"What I have to tell you," he went on, "is that Euphus and I had a little time to look in some books. It was while we were waiting for our chance to escape from those meddlesome reporters."

"UNFAIR!" Miss Ogelthorpe burst out, standing up and shouting across the table. "I PROTEST such an unfair statement."

"It's a familiar accusation," the Mayor sighed, talking to Miss Pickerell. "I hear it regularly at City Council meetings."

"The shouting is much louder at our bazaar-sale meetings," Miss Pickerell informed him.

"What did you say?" the Governor demanded.

"What did you say, Miss Pickerell? I can't hear you! But never mind for the moment! Are you about to go on, Professor?"

"I apologize," Professor Humwhistel said to Miss Ogelthorpe. "And I will go on, Governor. As I was saying, we referred to some books. Euphus examined the appropriate sections in my zoology books. And I pored over the taxonomy books. Nowhere did we find even a hint of a clue. We saw no pictures of a mouse resembling this animal. We read nothing that could be a description of such an animal."

"It's still a mouse," Dr. Haggerty said, smiling and looking very relaxed.

Deputy Administrator Blakely scowled.

"You owe us an explanation, Dr. Haggerty," he said. "A very thorough explanation."

"Certainly," Dr. Haggerty replied. "Euphus will give it to you."

"Euphus!" everybody around the table exclaimed.

"Euphus," Dr. Haggerty repeated. "He told me his theory while we were waiting for the Mayor and the Governor to arrive and for Professor Humwhistel to return from a telephone call he was making in the outer office. The theory is perfectly valid and supports my opinion that what we have here sleeping on the Deputy Administrator's conference table is unquestionably a mouse."

The Mayor murmured that it was getting very hot in the room. He rolled up his shirt-sleeves. The

43

Governor began nervously stroking his moustache. Mr. Blakely glared at Euphus. Rosemary nudged her brother. Euphus stood up and walked to the head of the table. He took a book out of a pocket in his rumpled plaid jacket and let his eyes wander slowly around the room. Miss Pickerell wondered for a moment whether he might not change his mind about becoming a scientist someday and go on the stage instead.

"It's a matter of isolation," he began, "a matter of geographic isolation."

"Of course," Professor Humwhistel mumbled unhappily. "I should also have referred to my books on geographic isolation."

"It wasn't your fault, Professor," Euphus said. "You didn't have the time. And you were too worried about the animal to think of everything."

Miss Pickerell had never known Euphus to be so polite before. Her mind began to turn to the idea of a political career for him. Professor Humwhistel didn't seem to be considering any such notion. He asked Euphus to continue.

"We've been studying about geographic isolation in school," Euphus went on. "And my science teacher told us about the squirrels near the Grand Canyon. The Kaibab squirrels on the north side have a black belly and a pure white tail. But their relatives, on the south side, have a white belly and their tails are white only on the underside. This book tells all about it, too."

Euphus paused to hold up the book. Dr. Haggerty gestured for him to go on.

"It happened this way because of the Grand Canyon, which the squirrels could not cross," he added. "And after many generations, the evolutionary process took over."

"What do you mean by the evolutionary process took over?" the Governor demanded. "Can you explain that, Euphus?"

"Yes, sir," Euphus said. "It happens lots of times. There's the kangaroo, for example. Kangaroos live only in Australia."

"I believe Australia separated from Asia many years ago," the Governor remarked.

"Seventy MILLION years ago," Euphus told him.

"And during this time," Professor Humwhistel stated, "the mammals on this island continent evolved independently of, and differently from, those on the Asian mainland. And . . ."

"Very differently," Euphus interrupted. "The mammals in Australia have pouches in which they bring up their babies. ALL the mammals, the kangaroos, the koala bears, all of them! My science teacher says it's geographic isolation making for a different evolution."

"What has all this got to do with the animal *here?*" Deputy Administrator Blakely protested, staring hard at Euphus, Professor Humwhistel, and Dr. Haggerty, each in turn.

"It's the same process," Dr. Haggerty stood up to say. "That's . . ."

"That's what may have happened to the mouse," Euphus broke in again, raising his voice above Dr. Haggerty's. "That's why he has a different kind of fur and different-looking ears and . . ."

"Not HE," Dr. Haggerty corrected. "SHE! This mouse is a girl."

"I've named her Ellie," Rosemary called out, "because of her ears. They hang down like an elephant's."

Professor Humwhistel gave her a very absent-minded smile.

"What we still need to know," he stated gravely, "is where this animal lived. What *barriers* existed that made it impossible for her to leave her own restricted environment and to develop in the way that she did? In other words, where does she come from?"

Dr. Haggerty and Euphus said nothing. Neither did anybody else. It was the Mayor who finally broke the silence.

"One thing's for sure," he said. "That animal did not come from outer space. No planet in outer space would be silly enough to send a mouse as its first ambassador to the planet Earth."

"It's certainly no way to develop good interplanetary relationships," the Governor agreed, nodding emphatically. "No way at all."

"Well," Mr. Blakely said, "if she's not from

outer space, my responsibility is over. And so is this meeting."

"What about Ellie?" Miss Pickerell screamed, as chairs began to scrape and people started moving away from the table. "What should we do about Ellie?"

Deputy Administrator Blakely shrugged his shoulders.

Miss Pickerell looked from face to face, searching for someone to say something. Only Dr. Haggerty looked back at her.

"She needs a good home," he said quietly. "A home with lots of love and understanding."

All eyes turned instantly to Miss Pickerell.

"She's perfectly healthy," Dr. Haggerty went on. "A bit bedraggled at the moment, but she'll get over that. And she won't be any trouble."

"You're forgetting about another part of this geographic evolutionary process," Professor Humwhistel, looking strangely worried, reminded him. "You're forgetting about the trouble associated with separating the species member away from its own environment. We must consider . . ."

Miss Pickerell wondered what the Professor meant. But nobody was listening. Excited exclamations were coming from everyone.

"I'll come and feed her, even after I go back home," Rosemary offered. "Every single day, I promise."

"Sunflower seeds make an excellent diet," Dr. Haggerty said.

"But Pumpkins . . . and Sampson . . . ," Miss Pickerell spluttered. "And even Nancy Agatha . . ."

"They'll get used to her," Dr. Haggerty said. "And . . ."

It was at just this moment that the mouse squealed. Rosemary rushed to pick her up, then walked back to put her gently in Miss Pickerell's hands.

"The poor little thing," Miss Pickerell whispered, looking tenderly down at her. "So far from home! And hungry, too, I'm sure! Was it sunflower seeds that you recommended, Dr. Haggerty?"

Professor Humwhistel escorted Miss Pickerell out of the office. He still had the strange, worried expression on his face when he helped her into her automobile.

5
ELLIE, THE
ELEPHANT-EARED
MOUSE, GLIDES

The *Square Toe Gazette* published daily bulletins about everything that was happening to Ellie. The bulletins were printed in extra-large letters in a box-like space on the upper right-hand side of the very front page. They told how much Ellie weighed every day and how her long ears were becoming more erect and more beautiful all the time. Miss Ogelthorpe's name always appeared on the bottom as a signature.

Rosemary, who weighed the mouse regularly and neatly copied the numbers from the kitchen scale onto a large chart posted on the refrigerator door, insisted that she never gave any of this information to Miss Ogelthorpe. Euphus laughed when Miss Pickerell asked him if he gave Miss Ogelthorpe her facts. He was much too busy with his school science work to bother with the lady reporter, he said. Miss Pickerell couldn't figure it out until she remembered that Miss Ogelthorpe was very friendly with her neighbor, Mrs. Broadribb, and that Mrs. Broadribb was even friendlier with Miss Lemon. *And* Mrs. Broadribb walked into the kitchen almost every morning to ask about Ellie, while she sat at the table drinking coffee and spreading raspberry jam on a muffin.

On Mondays, Wednesdays, and Fridays, the *Square Toe Gazette* also printed a story that Miss Ogelthorpe wrote about Ellie. It took up two whole newspaper columns and was the subject of conversation all over Square Toe City. Miss Pickerell could not even go into the supermarket without hearing somebody talking about it.

Miss Ogelthorpe was very proud of all her stories. She was particularly proud of the one she called BIRDS IN THEIR NESTS AGREE.

"I got the idea for the title from a poem I once read," she explained to Miss Pickerell when she came up to the farm to give her some extra copies she had saved for her. "I think it describes perfectly how Ellie and Pumpkins and Sampson and Nancy Agatha get along with each other."

"I suppose it does," Miss Pickerell agreed thoughtfully. "Pumpkins hissed when I first introduced Ellie to him. It was a very short hiss. I sometimes think he made that unpleasant sound because he believed it was expected of him. Pumpkins is a very cooperative cat."

"Oh!" Miss Ogelthorpe exclaimed. "How I

wish you had given me that information before I wrote the story! It would have added such a special touch."

"It's still a very nice story," Miss Pickerell said politely.

Miss Ogelthorpe smiled as she straightened her floppy spring hat and started to button her canary yellow coat in preparation for leaving.

"Mr. Clanghorn, our editor, thinks so, too," she said. "He has received dozens of letters and I can't begin to tell you how many telephone calls from readers about it. They keep telling him that they read the stories about Ellie even BEFORE they turn to the recipes or the news about births, deaths, and marriages. Can you imagine that, Miss Pickerell?"

Miss Pickerell certainly could. Her own telephone never stopped ringing. Mr. Kettelson and Professor Humwhistel called the most often. Mr. Kettelson usually ended his calls by asking how Ellie liked the box he had made for her to sleep and eat in. The Professor *always* ended *his* conversations by saying, "Be sure to call me, Miss Pickerell, should there be any trouble with Ellie." Miss Pickerell would invariably ask him what he meant by that statement, but his only answer was "Mmm." Sometimes, she could feel shivers running up and down her spine when he let out his long, drawn-out "Mmm."

Mr. Esticott, back on his job as train conductor because he could not stand being retired any longer, did more than telephone. He visited every day. He came in the early afternoon, just before he reported to work, and sat looking adoringly at Ellie. Ellie always sprang up to the edge of the table and made soft trilling sounds as she sat looking back at him.

"She's much bigger now, with her long whiskers and her fur all fluffed out," he kept commenting. "And her ears are not pressed against her face anymore. The way they were in the pictures those reporters took when she first floated into Square Toe City. My daughter noticed that the ears were actually tucked under her chin in one of the pictures."

"She folded them like a scarf for warmth," Miss Pickerell told him. "Dr. Haggerty explained that to me. But now she's not wet and cold anymore . . ."

"And I think she loves me," Mr. Esticott added eagerly. "She's pushing her head toward me so that I can pat it."

Miss Pickerell refrained from telling him that Ellie did this with everybody, everybody except Mrs. Broadribb, that is. Mrs. Broadribb's voice was much too loud for Ellie's taste and she definitely did not like the disturbing noise of Mrs. Broadribb's bird-watching glasses. Mrs. Broadribb always wore them on a chain around her neck, and they clanked when she took one of her frequent deep breaths.

Mr. Esticott often gave it as his opinion that

Ellie was one of the smartest and most alert animals he had ever met. He was sure of this when he saw her extend her long ears, as if they were the wings of an airplane, to help her jump from the table to a chair and from the chair to the floor.

"She's gliding!" he shouted. "Actually gliding!"

The very next Monday, Miss Ogelthorpe's story in the *Square Toe Gazette* was printed under the title ELLIE GLIDES. Mr. Esticott had described all the details to Mr. Kettelson over the telephone. Miss Lemon had lost no time in relaying them to Miss Ogelthorpe.

"I don't trust that young woman," Mr. Esticott said when Miss Pickerell explained to him about Miss Lemon. "I never did."

But then, Miss Pickerell reflected, Mr. Esticott rarely trusted anyone. He didn't even trust Dr. Haggerty when the doctor told Miss Pickerell that Ellie, who was no longer eating as much as she usually did, probably needed a change in her diet.

"She may be getting tired of the sunflower seeds," he said. "Animals like variety, the same as humans. I'll send along some other foods. And we won't worry yet."

"What did he mean by not worrying YET?" Mr. Esticott demanded when she repeated the conversation to him.

"There's nothing wrong with Ellie," Miss Pickerell replied heatedly. "She just needs a change from the sunflower seeds. I have to keep changing the food I give Pumpkins and Sampson, too. They don't want the same thing all the time, either."

Mr. Esticott said, "Humph!"

"And I told him," Miss Pickerell went on, "that her nose was cold and moist and that her underbelly was comfortably cool. Without a thermometer, that's how you find out whether an animal has fever or not. It's the same as what a mother does when she feels her child's forehead with the back of her hand."

Mr. Esticott ignored this remark.

"Do you remember when your cow was sick?" he asked.

"Certainly," Miss Pickerell told him. "I remember that you advised me to get sunglasses for her eyes. It was a ridiculous suggestion."

"But your cow WAS sick, wasn't she?" Mr. Esticott insisted.

Miss Pickerell was almost glad when the school that Euphus and Rosemary attended shut down because of a teachers' strike and their mother called to ask if they might return to the farm for a while. It would save them the trouble of taking the bus the way they'd been doing after school every day to visit Ellie.

"And I've warned them about using their radios and TVs and about picking up after themselves," their mother added. "I mean the clothes they're always dropping on the floor for someone else to pick up."

Miss Pickerell doubted that the warnings would do much good. But she was ready to welcome practically any distraction from Mr. Esticott.

Euphus and Rosemary arrived within the hour. Euphus had a knapsack slung over his shoulders. The leaves of a very tall plant stuck out from the top of the knapsack. Rosemary carried a large box and a cardboard mock-up of two plants standing opposite each other.

"It's my experiment," Euphus announced. "My experiment to learn whether Ellie is a field or a forest mouse."

"What difference would that make?" Miss Pickerell questioned.

"You *never* know," Euphus replied. "Even some of our greatest scientists don't always know where their experiments will lead."

Rosemary put the box down in the middle of the kitchen floor. Euphus placed the tall bushy plant that had been sticking out of his knapsack on one side in the box and a low-growing plant on the other side. Ellie, curious as always, jumped into the box. Miss Pickerell reached over immediately to take her out. She also shooed away Sampson, who had run in from the pasture and was standing on his hind legs to see what was going on in the box.

"It's not going to hurt them," Euphus objected. "The plants aren't poisonous. And I just want to see which one Ellie likes better."

Ellie showed her preference immediately. She turned her nose up at the low plant. She climbed up the bushy plant and began first to lick the leaves and then to gnaw at them.

"That means she's a forest mouse," Rosemary informed Miss Pickerell. "She's looking for food on the tall plant. It's mostly tall plants that grow in a forest."

"We have to make sure," Euphus said. "Scientists always double-check."

He replaced the live plants with the mock-up of the tall and short cardboard plants.

Ellie's reactions were the same. She selected the tall plant again. And when she saw that she could not eat the tall cardboard plant, she jumped out of the box to find the real one.

"Forevermore!" Miss Pickerell whispered. "I must call Dr. Haggerty about this."

Dr. Haggerty was delighted.

"Nonpoisonous plants are good for an animal's digestion," he said. "Cut some of the leaves up for her, if you like. Either way, they may stimulate her appetite and help her regain that ounce in weight you said she lost last week."

The early morning edition of the *Square Toe Gazette* carried the story about the weight-loss in the *middle* of the front page. A banner headline asked the question IS ELLIE SICK? Miss Pickerell made up her mind never to talk to Miss Ogelthorpe or Miss Lemon again. She also wrote a letter to the *Square Toe Gazette* explaining that Ellie had lost only *half* an ounce. Mr. Esticott had nervously jiggled the scale when he weighed her. Rosemary had reweighed the mouse, discovered the error, and reported it to Dr. Haggerty.

"And I was too excited when I spoke to Dr. Haggerty to correct him," she added in a postscript to the letter. "But I fully expect the correction to appear in your very next edition."

Miss Pickerell felt too upset to write again to inquire why her letter was not printed the next day or the next or the next. Ellie had not regained even the half ounce of weight. And she did not glide around the house as much as she used to. On hot days, she simply sat very still, with her long ears extended on both sides. The ears also seemed to be losing some of their fur. But Dr. Haggerty explained that Ellie used her ears as a kind of air conditioner. The heat got radiated out from the thin skin to cool her off.

"I could have told you that," Euphus said. "And I can tell you about elephants, too. Elephants also use their large ears to keep them cool."

Dr. Haggerty's answer to Miss Pickerell's questions about Professor Humwhistel's repeated "Mmms" was not as thorough as his explanation about Ellie's ears.

"Unless there are definite signs to indicate it," he said, "I don't believe in looking ahead for trouble."

Miss Pickerell felt very relieved. She felt even more so when she saw Ellie asleep high up on Sampson's chest, her head resting contentedly under his chin and one of her own arms curled up in a small embrace. Actually, Miss Pickerell felt so relaxed that she decided to go on with the unfinished scarf she was knitting for Rosemary.

"And it's about time, too," she told herself, her needles clicking busily away while she watched Pumpkins walk haughtily past the sleeping dog and mouse to see what he could do about tangling up some of her knitting wool.

6
ELLIE HAS
A DEPRESSION

When Mr. Kettelson came up to the farm, Miss Pickerell entertained him in her parlor. She knew that it was his favorite room in the house.

"I'm sorry I couldn't get here before," he said as soon as he had made his usual admiring comments about the lemon polish she used on her furniture and about the pink lace curtains she had hanging on the windows. "But with that spring cold I had, I was flat on my back. I told the doctor I thought it might be the flu."

"Oh?" Miss Pickerell asked.

"He didn't agree or disagree," Mr. Kettelson explained. "He just told me to keep on the aspirin routine until my temperature went down. That was nearly three weeks ago. I've been feeling a little dizzy ever since, and I've had to hire an assistant for the shop."

Miss Pickerell made some very sympathetic sounds.

"But about Ellie," Mr. Kettelson went on. "I've seen nothing about her in the *Square Toe Gazette* lately."

"Naturally," Miss Pickerell replied immediately. "I believe I told you over the telephone that I no longer permit Miss Ogelthorpe to enter my house."

"And Ellie . . . ?" Mr. Kettelson persisted.

"She's gone back to eating the sunflower seeds," Miss Pickerell replied, sighing. "But only out of Rosemary's hand. And only a few at a time."

"Most animals don't eat much in warm weather," Mr. Kettelson said encouragingly. "You told me that yourself once, Miss Pickerell, when Pumpkins and Sampson weren't eating a lot and you were worried."

Miss Pickerell made no reply. She was looking out of the open windows. The lace curtains were billowing in the spring breeze and she was able to see her middle nephew, Euphus, trampling heedlessly over her newly planted cucumber patch as he raced toward the kitchen door. She also observed that he was trying to balance a load of magazines with glossy covers on them against his chest. Mr. Kettelson waved to Euphus.

"I have to go back now, Miss Pickerell," he said, pulling himself up from his seat on the horsehair sofa. "My assistant knows only how to collect his wages. He doesn't bother to explain the merchandise to customers or to give them reasons why they should buy. Things are definitely NOT what they used to be!"

Miss Pickerell could only agree with this sentiment. In the supermarket, there was no one to help her find what she wanted to buy. Why, she even had to weigh things for herself.

"What is this world coming to?" she asked.

She and Mr. Kettelson sighed together. Mr. Kettelson said that he would stop in the pasture to say hello to Nancy Agatha before he ran to catch his bus, and that he would be back to visit again very soon.

It was half past twelve when Miss Pickerell returned to her kitchen. The whole morning gone and she hadn't even gotten around to polishing the brasses she had piled up on the table! Euphus had transferred them to the countertop, she saw. He had spread his magazines out there instead.

"There's a picture of me in this one," he said, lifting one up for her to look at. "It's a picture of me and the Governor. The Governor asked the City Hall reporters to take it when he came back from the State Capital yesterday. He said a picture of him at City Hall was important."

"Very nice," Miss Pickerell commented, not even troubling to ask how Euphus got into the picture. He always seemed to be there, wherever that was, when something was happening.

"And here's what the Governor said to the reporters," Euphus went on. "It's printed right under the picture. I'll read it to you."

"I can read it for myself," Miss Pickerell replied.

She skimmed over the Governor's statement, which took up almost the entire half of the magazine page. She reread the part in the middle where the Governor talked about how the country's wildlife was being threatened by *cruel and ruthless extinction.*

"He's absolutely right," she paused to say to Euphus. "All those innocent animals, their lives just snuffed out that way. There ought to be some . . ."

"Read the part that you skipped," Euphus urged. "He talks about you there."

Miss Pickerell lowered her eyes to the paper again.

"And," the Governor was saying, "as Chief Executive of this great State, I want to express my concern about our endangered species and certainly about Ellie, who may be the only surviving member of her kind. Fortunately, she was rescued by our own gallant Miss Pickerell."

"There's another statement from the Governor at the back," Euphus stated, quickly turning the pages. "He talks about some of the animals that need protection. He mentions the panda and the tiger and the rhino and the snow leopard. . . . I guess he got their names out of a book."

Miss Pickerell's mind nearly reeled at this outrageous statement. She simply HAD to do something about Euphus's behavior.

"The Governor knows about a great many things that you are not aware of, Euphus," she said sternly. "He is also entitled to respect. I've been meaning to talk to you about your manners. Lately, they have . . ."

Miss Pickerell had no chance to go on with her lecture. Rosemary, cupping the mouse in her hands, raced into the kitchen.

"Ellie won't eat," she cried. "Not even when I let her pick the sunflower seeds out of my hand the way she likes, instead of from her saucer. She wouldn't eat them last night or this morning, either. And look at her, Aunt Lavinia!"

Miss Pickerell stared, openmouthed. Ellie had changed for the worse. Her eyes, always so bright and alert, were now dull and a little aimless. The soft, pretty shine was almost gone from her fur. She seemed even to have shrunk somewhat, Miss Pickerell thought.

"Nonsense!" she told herself. "It's her position in Rosemary's hands that's giving me that impression."

She quickly revised that opinion when she took a closer look. She paused only to push her glasses up before running across her freshly scrubbed kitchen floor to telephone Dr. Haggerty.

"He'll know what to do," she said to Euphus and Rosemary as her fumbling fingers dialed the

letter "O" for the operator. "He'll come right over and he'll examine her and . . ."

Dr. Haggerty listened carefully when she told him all about what was happening. But he said only that he would call her back.

Miss Pickerell sat down next to the telephone to wait. She made a cradle out of her hands and rocked Ellie the way she had rocked her seven nieces and nephews when they were babies. She kept stroking her head and telling her that help was on the way, would soon be here, very soon, very, very soon, while she waited for the telephone to ring.

The seconds passed. The minutes passed. Euphus, Rosemary, and Miss Pickerell sat staring at the clock. The only sound in the room was the quiet ticking that resounded over and over again in Miss Pickerell's head. It was 1:25 P.M. when the ringing at the front door suddenly shattered the almost unbelievable silence. Miss Pickerell nearly stumbled as she flew through the kitchen, pantry, and parlor to the front of the house. Dr. Haggerty was standing on the doorstep. Professor Humwhistel was walking behind him. They were busy arguing with each other.

"I know," Dr. Haggerty was telling the angry-looking Professor, "I should have listened when you tried to warn me. I saw that expression on your face."

"You knew as well as I about the difficulties of separating a species member away from its own environment," Professor Humwhistel said, "and about how the difficulties are even greater where geographic isolation is involved. If only for Miss Pickerell's sake, you should have listened! To spare her the heartache!"

"I was hoping," Dr. Haggerty murmured. "Hoping against hope that it would work out. Frankly, what was the alternative?"

"Well, you'd better take a look to make sure," Professor Humwhistel advised as he took Ellie out of Miss Pickerell's hands and laid her down on Pumpkins' favorite pillow in the overstuffed chair near a window. "You'll have enough light here, I believe."

Dr. Haggerty picked up the battered black bag he had dropped on the floor and took out the tiny instruments he used when people brought him their hamsters, gerbils, and guinea pigs to examine. Miss Pickerell watched him sterilize the tiny thermometer in a bottle of alcohol before he began.

His examination of Ellie was quick but thorough. He took her temperature, looked down her throat, peered into her eyes through a magnifying glass, held his stethoscope against the front and back of her chest, and tested both her blood pressure and her reflexes.

To Miss Pickerell, it seemed like an eternity before he looked up to say anything. And then, he spoke to Professor Humwhistel.

"It's just as you thought," he told him. "Organically, she's normal."

When he turned to Miss Pickerell, he said there was a lot to talk about.

"We'd better sit down," he suggested.

"Not here," Miss Pickerell whispered, gesturing toward the door.

Professor Humwhistel had forgotten to close it behind him. Mrs. Broadribb, her ample bosom heaving with excitement, and the bird-watching glasses banging against her chest, stood just outside. Miss Ogelthorpe was right next to her. Mrs. Broadribb led the way in and beckoned for Miss Ogelthorpe to follow, when Miss Pickerell began walking back into her kitchen.

It felt like another eternity before Dr. Haggerty spoke again. He sat in Miss Pickerell's rocker, holding Ellie on his lap and propelling himself back and forth while Miss Pickerell stood trembling before him.

"I don't know exactly how I can explain this to you, Miss Pickerell," he said finally. "I suppose the best way is to tell you that Ellie is suffering from a depression."

"I know all about depressions," Mrs. Broadribb remarked loudly from where she was now standing near the broom closet. "My late husband had headaches that the doctor said came from his depression. What he was so sad about, I will never know."

Miss Ogelthorpe commented that it was too bad about Mrs. Broadribb's late husband.

"And," Mrs. Broadribb continued, "Mr. Esticott has told a number of friends about the depression that he had. It was retirement that made him feel that way, he said. That's why he came back to work as a train conductor. Mr. Esticott doesn't believe in retirement for anyone."

Miss Pickerell was nearly boiling with rage. All of this was definitely beside the point, and she had no hesitation about saying as much to both Mrs. Broadribb and the lady reporter.

"What's more," she added to Dr. Haggerty, "I don't see how Ellie could possibly be depressed. It isn't as if she were left alone in a kennel for weeks on end, the way some people do with their animals, and Mrs. Broadribb knows exactly the ones I mean. Dr. Haggerty had even warned them that some animals can get very depressed under such circumstances."

Dr. Haggerty did not reply. Miss Pickerell took Ellie from his lap.

"It's the loss of weight I'm concerned about," she said, ignoring Dr. Haggerty and talking to Professor Humwhistel as she showed him how two small bones were beginning to show through Ellie's fur. "I've heard about animal malnutrition . . ."

"Malnutrition?" Miss Ogelthorpe burst out. "After the way you've been feeding her, Miss Pickerell! You described the diet to me. Of course, after your letter to the editor, I didn't dare to write up the story. But I have my notes on it here, somewhere."

She rummaged hastily in her bag. A lipstick, a

green ball-point pen, and a half-finished bar of chocolate fell out as she searched.

"Ah! Here it is!" she announced, dragging out a crumpled sheet of paper and reading from it: "A medium-size meal at breakfast, a large one for lunch, a smaller one for supper, and, if she still seemed hungry, a bedtime snack."

"Aunt Lavinia changed that diet," Rosemary called out. "She changed it to on-demand feeding when I reminded her that I was raised that way. Ellie had her sunflower seeds whenever she asked for them. And *anything else* that Dr. Haggerty recommended."

Dr. Haggerty smiled sadly.

"You took excellent care of her, Miss Pickerell," he said. "Ellie has lost her appetite and is beginning to lose weight only because she is lonely."

Miss Pickerell stared, dumbfounded.

"How can she be lonely?" she pleaded. "Somebody is always playing with her, even Pumpkins, who started to spit when I first introduced them. And Nancy Agatha loves having her as company in the barn. And Sampson is so good-natured, he lets her ride on his back. I can call him in from the pasture and show . . ."

"She's lonely for her own home," Professor Humwhistel interrupted quietly. "For the animals who live in that home and are her fellow creatures."

"You remember the fawn?" Dr. Haggerty asked.

Miss Pickerell remembered only too well the

wounded fawn that Dr. Haggerty had adopted and made a pet of. But Dr. Haggerty's love hadn't helped. The fawn still wanted to return to the wild.

"Like the fawn," Professor Humwhistel said, "Ellie waited only until she felt well again to start yearning for home."

"It's too soon, too soon," Miss Pickerell cried out. "The fawn waited longer."

"She needed more time to get well again," Dr. Haggerty said. "Ellie can't wait much longer."

"You . . . you mean she may not survive . . . ?" Miss Pickerell began.

"How can she when she doesn't eat?" Rosemary wailed.

"All sorts of complications set in with serious depressions," Dr. Haggerty said. "More and more bad illnesses are diagnosed today as being related to depression."

"I'm afraid you'll have to take her back to her home," Professor Humwhistel told her. "There's no other solution."

"I have to think! I have to think!" Miss Pickerell murmured.

"Back to her home?" Mrs. Broadribb shouted from where she was now leaning against the sink. "How can you do that, Miss Pickerell, when you DON'T EVEN KNOW where that home is?"

"I know," Euphus shouted back. "I figured it out."

7

"I WILL FIND ELLIE'S HOME"

Miss Pickerell threw her middle nephew a very startled glance. He had been so quiet, she had almost forgotten that he was in the room.

"What did you figure out?" she asked instantly.

"Well," Euphus said, moving off the telephone stool and closer to Miss Pickerell at the table, "I remembered that Ellie and the tree she was clutching were floating DOWNSTREAM when they came into Square Toe City."

"We all know that," Dr. Haggerty commented.

"So," Euphus continued, "if we want to take her back where she came from, we have to go UPSTREAM."

"UP that terrible river," Rosemary cried out. "I wouldn't dare!"

"Neither would I," Mrs. Broadribb volunteered. "Mr. Esticott once told me that a cousin of his was actually drowned in that river."

"NEARLY drowned was what Mr. Esticott said," Miss Ogelthorpe told her. "And when I went to the cousin to get the story for the newspaper, he said that even that wasn't entirely accurate. He said that he nearly slipped when he was walking along the edge of the river."

"Be that as it may," Mrs. Broadribb persisted, "it is still a raging river that overflowed and flooded our . . ."

"It isn't raging anymore," Miss Pickerell stated.

"There is still a strong current," Professor Humwhistel observed. "A very strong current!"

Euphus did not seem to hear the Professor's remark.

"And," he went on, talking to Miss Pickerell, "somewhere along that river is Ellie's real home. I don't know exactly where yet, but I'm figuring that out, too."

"I will search for it, INCH BY INCH," Miss Pickerell said, still stroking the mouse who now lay half asleep in her lap. "I will find Ellie's home. I will NOT let poor little Ellie die of loneliness."

Miss Pickerell did not go on talking. She was giving her attention to the sound of a motorcycle definitely coming up her private road. She could hear the whirr distinctly as it came closer, and there was no mistaking the roaring, sputtering noise it made when it came to a stop outside her farmyard gate.

"Mercy!" she exclaimed when she looked out of her window and saw that it was Assistant Sheriff Stella T. Swiftlee sitting at the wheel, and that the Mayor was crouching in the sidecar at her right.

"I have just heard about Ellie," the Mayor said the minute that he and the Assistant Sheriff finished crossing the back garden and entered the kitchen. "I came as fast as I could. Our Assistant Sheriff was kind enough to offer me a ride on her motorcycle."

Assistant Sheriff Swiftlee smiled briefly. She smoothed down the skirt of her bright blue uniform and removed a speck of dust from one of the gleaming brass buttons on her jacket.

"We made the trip in ten minutes," she said as she checked her wristwatch. "It is only a little after one o'clock now. What is the matter with Ellie, Miss Pickerell?"

"She's pining for her home in the wilderness," Miss Ogelthorpe explained, looking up for a moment from the notes she was making on her pad. "Miss Pickerell is journeying up the river to take her there."

"I have been led to believe," Mrs. Broadribb announced, "that the river becomes more perilous the farther upstream one goes. It may even be impenetrable at some points."

Miss Pickerell did not answer. She was looking down at the mouse.

"Somewhere up there," she murmured to her, "we will find the lost world that is your home. And you'll be all well and happy again."

"Of course she will," Rosemary, standing next to Miss Pickerell, whispered.

"I don't think it's so dangerous," Euphus piped up, talking to the Mayor. "And, anyway, Aunt Lavinia wasn't afraid when she was crossing the ocean in a balloon or when she . . ."

Professor Humwhistel interrupted him with a very loud sigh. Miss Pickerell let out a sigh of her own. She wasn't about to take the time to tell Euphus that it was the North Sea, not really the ocean, or to remind him about the times she had fainted on some of her other journeys. And he already knew about how terrified she was of climbing ladders and of riding up in express elevators and of going down on escalators. She was just getting ready to mention this to Professor Humwhistel, when the Mayor spoke to her.

"I am sorry, Miss Pickerell," he said, "that I cannot accompany you. Unfortunately, we, the City Labor Unions and I, that is, are scheduled to continue our talks regarding the next union contracts. You know how important that is, especially the contract with the teachers."

Euphus and Rosemary groaned.

"But, to TAKE MY PLACE," the Mayor added, as he smiled at Miss Ogelthorpe, "I am now delegating Assistant Sheriff Swiftlee, who will protect you EVERY MOMENT of the way. AND I am sure that our most efficient lady reporter who, I notice, is now very busy with her pad and her pencil, will be happy to hear about this decision."

Mrs. Broadribb's mouth fell open. The Assistant Sheriff looked astonished.

"But how," she asked after a moment, "how are we to go up the river, Your Honor? We need transport of some sort, and . . ."

"The City launch," the Mayor answered, before anyone else could say a word. "I will let you have the new City launch. When do you plan to leave, Miss Pickerell?"

"The sooner the better," Dr. Haggerty murmured as he leaned down to look again at the sleeping Ellie. "Perhaps right now would be best."

Miss Pickerell knew what he meant.

"I will go now," she said. "I will stop only to let Pumpkins and Sampson and Nancy Agatha say good-bye to their friend. They will never see her again."

Pumpkins and Sampson ran to meet her from the pasture. They seemed to understand, and licked Ellie's small white paws when Miss Pickerell showed her to them. And Nancy Agatha mooed what sounded like a protest. Miss Pickerell had to take a very firm hold on herself when she tried to explain that she was doing this for Ellie's good.

On her way back, Miss Pickerell stopped at the barn to let Ellie, now awake, take a last look at the box that Mr. Kettelson had built for her.

"This is where you ate and slept while you were

here with us," Miss Pickerell said as Ellie sniffed at the box. "I hope you will always remember how happy you were here and how happy you made us, too."

The tears were streaming down Miss Pickerell's face when she walked into her kitchen again. Rosemary was sobbing out loud.

"I hate good-byes," she said, clutching Ellie to her for a last brief hug. "I HATE them!"

Miss Pickerell nodded weakly.

"But I'll take care of Pumpkins and Sampson and Nancy Agatha," Rosemary went on. "And I'll call Mr. Kettelson, the way you always tell me to, if there's any problem. And . . . and you'll be home soon."

"Very soon," Miss Pickerell promised. "Maybe even later today."

"We hope," Professor Humwhistel said sadly.

The Mayor, finishing two very fast telephone calls, advised Miss Pickerell that everything was arranged. He had ordered a limousine for her from the nearest taxi service. And the City launch stood ready and waiting. He and Assistant Sheriff Swiftlee would meet her at the pier.

Dr. Haggerty, patting Ellie's head, offered to let Miss Pickerell have one of his animal carriers to transport the mouse. Miss Pickerell refused.

"No," she said, "I carried Ellie in my knitting bag when I brought her to the farm. And I will carry her in the bag now. It will be more familiar to her and less frightening."

She put on the hat and mauve jacket that she took out of the hallway closet and snatched up the umbrella and knitting bag that were lying on a chair.

"Come, Ellie," Miss Pickerell said, as she settled her gently into the bag. "We're going home."

Mrs. Broadribb ran after her when she started walking out of the door.

"Wait!" she shouted. "Take my bird-watching glasses. They may come in handy somewhere."

She slipped the chain around Miss Pickerell's neck. Miss Pickerell thanked her.

Miss Ogelthorpe, now in back of Mrs. Broadribb, was dabbing at her eyes with a piece of purple tissue.

"I wish there was something I could do, as well," she said.

Miss Pickerell thanked her, too.

"Come," the Mayor urged. "I see that the limousine has arrived."

He took her arm and walked with her across the lawn and up to a waiting car. Euphus was already there, sitting next to the uniformed chauffeur.

"I'm going," he said. "It was my idea. And I'm the one who knows about geographic isolation. That will be MUCH more important than those silly bird-watching glasses you have on."

The Mayor looked questioningly at Miss Pickerell. She stared at Euphus. He always managed to go *somewhere* with her because of his superior understanding of science. She shrugged her shoulders. The Mayor did the same. He guided her into the back of the car, waved to her, and jumped up to join Assistant Sheriff Swiftlee on the motorcycle.

8
UP THE
RAGING RIVER

Miss Pickerell was completely taken aback when she saw who was sitting at the engine in the front part of the launch. It was young Mr. Gilhuly, the red-headed, freckle-faced postman who put the mail in her Rural Free Delivery box promptly at 9:00 A.M. every day. Sometimes, when he thought it might be important, he also made a special trip up the mountain to hand a letter to her on a weekend or a holiday.

"Good afternoon, Mr. Gilhuly," she said, stopping to speak to him before stepping up on the launch. "I had no idea you were coming along on this trip."

"Neither did I until a little while ago," Mr. Gilhuly admitted. "I'm what the Mayor calls an emergency pilot. He couldn't get anybody else on such short notice. And, oh yes, I nearly forgot—

there was an urgent call on his beeper and he had to run off, Miss Pickerell. He said to wish you good luck."

Mr. Gilhuly leaned out to look sympathetically at Miss Pickerell's knitting bag.

"I hope I can help you find Ellie's home," he added.

Miss Pickerell opened the bag to let him see the mouse. Ellie was completely awake now. But she put her paws over her eyes when Miss Pickerell kept the bag open.

"It's probably the sun that bothers her," Mr. Gilhuly suggested. "You'd better go into the back with her. There's an awning over the back half of the launch. Like the one you have on your trailer, Miss Pickerell. This one is striped, though. Well, we'd better get going."

But before Mr. Gilhuly had time to start the engine, there was a screeching of brakes on the shore. The Governor, shiny top hat in hand, was leaping out of his official State car.

"I heard," he explained between gasps as he tried to catch his breath, "I heard from Miss Lemon. About your report to Dr. Haggerty. And about Dr. Haggerty's conversation with Professor Humwhistel right after that. I came as fast as I could."

"Oh!" Miss Pickerell, also gasping, exclaimed.

"It would have been sooner," the Governor went on, "if I hadn't needed to stay and finish the State Budget report. But never let it be said that the Governor of our great State hesitated in offering his assistance when it was needed."

"I am sure of that, Governor," Miss Pickerell told him.

"And," the Governor continued, "the moment Miss Lemon called and told me about your trip, I made up my mind. I will join you in your brave search, Miss Pickerell. It is the least I can do."

The Governor followed Miss Pickerell to the back of the launch, where Assistant Sheriff Swiftlee and Euphus were already sitting on striped canvas chairs. Miss Pickerell sat down next to Euphus and looked around just as Mr. Gilhuly started the engine. The launch was smaller than she had thought it would be. And it was furnished in a way she had not expected, either. It had a red carpet on the floor, a counter with glasses and all kinds of bottles on it in a corner, and a large, gilt-framed mirror above the counter. She sat thinking about how the launch reminded her of a yacht she had seen on a television news program a few weeks ago. The yacht belonged to a prince or an emperor, she couldn't remember just which. Whoever he was, he seemed to be very important, and the news program showed him traveling on the yacht to an international peace conference. Miss Pickerell remarked to Assistant Sheriff Swiftlee that she was very puzzled about the resemblance of the launch to the yacht on the television screen.

"The Mayor bought the launch after he saw that program," the Assistant Sheriff informed her.

"The City Council voted to give him the money when he explained what a good impression a launch furnished like the yacht would make on visiting officials. And he described how he would be able to show them the entire city from a river view on the launch."

"I understand he bought it at a very reduced price," the Governor muttered. "Personally, I am inclined to think that it was reduced *too* much. There are probably a number of defects that he didn't bother to examine it for."

"Oh!" Miss Pickerell breathed, listening closely for the sound of the engine.

But it seemed to be chugging away quite happily. And Mr. Gilhuly, his postman's cap now perched on the back of his head, did not look the least bit concerned. Miss Pickerell decided that the Governor was being unnecessarily alarmed. She turned her attention to Ellie.

The mouse, she saw, when she peered into the knitting bag, was awake and busily gnawing away at a small paper packet. Miss Pickerell recognized it immediately.

"The sunflower seeds I left on the table!" she exclaimed. "And Rosemary remembered!"

Rosemary had also put in a zippered bag full of sandwiches, a plastic bottle with Miss Pickerell's favorite peppermintade inside, and a note saying that she hoped the peppermintade would not be too warm by the time Miss Pickerell got around to drinking it.

"What a thoughtful child she is!" Miss Pickerell said to herself. "If only she weren't so timid. I can't imagine why she was afraid to go out on this river. It's as calm as it can be. And even Ellie doesn't seem to mind the ride."

But Ellie was not really as happy as Miss Pickerell had hoped. The mouse had managed to make a small hole in the paper packet and to draw a few seeds out with her paw. She sat sniffing at them. Not once, Miss Pickerell observed, did she open her mouth to eat any.

Miss Pickerell was beginning to feel less cheerful about the weather, too. She noticed a definite shift in the wind. Nobody else seemed at all concerned about it, however, least of all the Governor, who usually worried about all sorts of things.

"Where do you expect to find Ellie's home?" he was now asking.

"In some unknown world," Euphus replied shortly.

The Governor's eyebrows rose a little.

"Will you repeat that, Euphus?" he asked.

"That's what Professor Humwhistel said," Euphus answered, looking up for a moment from his book on geographic isolation, which he never seemed to stop reading.

"An UNKNOWN WORLD!" the Governor said, shuddering. "It could turn out to be like a nightmare, full of demons or monsters and all kinds of evil spirits."

Miss Pickerell felt the butterflies beginning to churn in her stomach. She had known a few nightmares of her own and they very much resembled what the Governor was describing. There was one she was able to remember because she had had it more than once. In this dream, a witch was pressing down on her chest and making it impossible for her to breathe. She nearly choked all over again with the very memory of the horror. And she shivered, as well, when Mr. Gilhuly pointed to the towering mountains ahead.

"Look at them!" he called out. "THOSE are my idea of a nightmare."

Miss Pickerell felt inclined to agree with him when she inspected the scene, first through Mrs. Broadribb's bird-watching glasses and then, when she couldn't bear the closeness of the sight anymore, without them. The mountains presented a most forbidding prospect. A few of them had some scrubby-looking trees growing here and there. Most of them were only huge walls of rock rising up on both sides of the river. They were not in the least like Square Toe Mountain, with its gentle curves and fresh-smelling trees and even flowers in the spring and summer times. And the launch was now entering a deep canyon, which grew darker and darker as Mr. Gilhuly kept the boat steadily moving upstream. Miss Pickerell shivered again. Assistant Sheriff Swiftlee, who had borrowed Mrs. Broadribb's bird-watching glasses and was now returning them, let out an exceptionally long sigh.

"Where do you propose to start looking for Ellie's home, Euphus?" she asked. "Around here, perhaps?"

Euphus closed his book with a resigned sigh of his own.

"I don't think so," he said. "There has to be a forest, of course, because Ellie is a forest mouse. But the forest has to be separated from the surrounding land by the BARRIER that Ellie could not cross. We haven't found that barrier yet. The forest . . ."

"Euphus conducted a test to determine that Ellie was a forest mouse," Miss Pickerell interrupted proudly.

"I can tell you about it," Euphus offered. "It involved finding out which plants . . ."

"The wind is shifting," Mr. Gilhuly suddenly shouted from the front of the launch. "It's shifting fast!"

The wind was certainly shifting, as she had suspected before, Miss Pickerell realized. And the river was narrowing and becoming swifter by the minute. The launch zigzagged on the water, from left to right, and forward and backward. Mr. Gilhuly, trying desperately to keep it moving upstream, could not stop it from being swept downstream when the waves dashed against it.

"I don't know what to do," he moaned. "I've never been an emergency pilot before."

"Where's the telephone?" the Governor shrieked. "We have to telephone for help!"

"The City Council didn't get around to voting on funds for a telephone," the Assistant Sheriff advised him. "But I have my two-way radio . . ."

She was already talking when the Governor screamed for her to add that it was raining, too, raining hard.

"And," she was reporting, "the river seems to be changing from moment to moment. The currents are creating rapids that are rising up against the front of the launch. The Governor has asked me to mention that it is also raining. But the rain is a secondary problem. The danger comes from the currents I described, the . . ."

"I can't navigate those currents," Mr. Gilhuly, the rain streaming from his cap and sodden uniform jacket, turned around to say.

Miss Pickerell, holding the knitting bag against her chest and whispering comforting words to Ellie, did not see how ANYBODY could possibly navigate such a frenzied outburst.

"We'll have to stop, Mr. Gilhuly," she said, hoping that she sounded a lot calmer than she felt. "We'll have to find a place."

"Right now!" the Governor ordered. "Stop RIGHT NOW!"

"How? Where?" Mr. Gilhuly cried. "I can't even see straight ahead of me."

He let go of the wheel as a wave taller than he was knocked him over. The unguided launch lurched perilously. The Assistant Sheriff and Euphus were both trying to get hold of the wheel, when the launch took a sudden leap into the air. Then, just as suddenly, it skidded sideways to land with a thud against a reedy, pebbly bank in what looked like the middle of nowhere.

9
THE MYSTERIOUS DRONING SOUND ON THE MOUNTAINTOP

The rain stopped almost as abruptly as it had started, though the sky was still black and threatening. From the position in which she landed after falling out of her chair, Miss Pickerell could see the thick, menacing clouds very clearly. But it was hard for her to see the other occupants of the launch.

Assistant Sheriff Swiftlee was the first person to move. She helped Miss Pickerell to get up and proceeded to shine her flashlight in every direction. Euphus lay sprawled under the corner table, his open book beside him. He refused to accept the hand that the Assistant Sheriff held out to him.

"That was some slide I took," he said, grinning from ear to ear as he crawled out. "The wind just knocked me over and then, WOW!"

The Assistant Sheriff made no reply. She was

too occupied with her search for Mr. Gilhuly and the Governor.

"Well, at least we're all here," she said when she spotted Mr. Gilhuly bending over the engine and the Governor looking as though he were glued to the chair that had landed not too far from Mr. Gilhuly. "And nobody seems very severely hurt."

"No bones broken, perhaps, but certainly uncomfortable," the Governor declared as he pulled himself out of the chair he was still gripping. "And my hat has been crushed, crushed beyond repair."

Mr. Gilhuly, wringing out his own postman's cap and jacket, offered to do the same with the Governor's hat. Euphus laughed until he had to stop to catch his breath. Miss Pickerell did not find Mr. Gilhuly's offer all that amusing. She refrained from expressing her opinion. She was giving her full attention to checking up on Ellie.

The mouse had retreated as far back as she could in the knitting bag. She had even managed to cover herself with the part of Rosemary's unfinished scarf that lay carefully folded up on the bottom. But she came out when Miss Pickerell called her name and she nuzzled the finger that Miss Pickerell held out to her. And, holding on to the finger, she stood up on her back legs and raised her elephantlike ears.

"We can't be too far from her home," Miss Pickerell murmured happily. "She's beginning to take an interest in her surroundings."

Euphus, who overheard her, nodded. He also yawned loudly.

"I'm hungry," he said. "Very hungry."

Miss Pickerell unzipped Rosemary's plastic bag. Assistant Sheriff Swiftlee helped her spread the sandwiches out on the counter. The Governor picked up the first one.

"Absolutely delicious!" he said as he bit into it.

Mr. Gilhuly and the Assistant Sheriff said they agreed. Miss Pickerell, munching on a sandwich and sipping some of the peppermintade, made a mental note to be sure to tell Rosemary about what everybody, especially the Governor, had said.

Mr. Gilhuly, finishing his third sandwich, opened his mouth to speak and closed it again. He walked resolutely behind the counter instead.

"My mother," he said, blushing beet-red under his freckles, "made me take some food along, too. She telephoned the Mayor first to make sure there was a kitchen, or what they call a galley, on the launch."

He stooped down to pick up a very large paper bag he had left there. Then he poured the contents out on the counter—two boxes of oatmeal cookies, a box of chocolate-covered doughnuts, one can of tea, one of instant coffee, one of instant chocolate, a carton of eggs, and a number of oranges.

"My mother likes for people to eat," Mr. Gilhuly said. "Especially me. She still thinks I'm a growing boy."

"I KNOW about mothers," Euphus burst out. "I can . . ."

Miss Pickerell definitely preferred for him NOT to go on.

"Euphus," she asked, interrupting, "was that a canyon that we entered? I thought . . ."

"It certainly was!" Euphus exclaimed immediately. "A canyon formed by erosion, the process by which the surface of the earth is worn away in some places by the action of wind and water. The eroded place usually becomes a deep valley with steep sides and often with a stream flowing through it."

"That certainly fits the bill here," Mr. Gilhuly said, looking up at the mountains on either side of the river.

"Well, the sky is all clear again," Miss Pickerell said, also looking up. "I believe I'll go out for a little walk."

"I'll go too," Mr. Gilhuly told her.

Euphus said he preferred to stay where he was and to consult some of the maps his pockets were always stuffed with. Assistant Sheriff Swiftlee thought she wanted to investigate the Mayor's galley facilities. The Governor announced that he was going to take a nap in one of the reclining beach chairs he saw folded up on the left side of the mirror.

"The river has become so very narrow," Miss Pickerell commented to Mr. Gilhuly as soon as they stepped off the launch.

"And just take a look at that sun," Mr. Gilhuly replied. "It resembles a round, red ball, hanging up there in the sky."

"I've seen it that way before," Miss Pickerell told him. "Usually for a little while, just before night falls."

She turned her attention to the river again. The rush of its relentless sweep forward was actually bending the partially submerged grasses that rose in its path. And the swollen waters were still slapping hard against the banks. It was not a very cheerful sight. Both Miss Pickerell and Mr. Gilhuly sighed and turned back.

They were retracing their steps to the launch, when Miss Pickerell paused to listen to a sound. It was a strange sound, more like an insistent drone than an actual noise. It lingered in the clear mountain air as an echo when it stopped. But it came two more times before, with a kind of rasp, it finally disappeared.

Mr. Gilhuly had no idea about what it could possibly be.

"I've never heard anything of that sort," he said. "Never!"

"I have," Miss Pickerell told him. "I wish . . . I wish I could remember where."

The sound kept going round and round in her head. Once, she almost felt the tip of her tongue getting ready to say what it was. But the words didn't come out when she opened her mouth. All the way back to the launch she kept racking her brains about it.

The Governor was fast asleep and snoring lightly when Miss Pickerell and Mr. Gilhuly stepped up on the launch again. Euphus was busy piling blankets on the rest of the beach chairs he had set up.

"They're for when we all go to sleep," he said. "I found them, the blankets, I mean, on the floor in a sort of alcove. That's where the galley is, too."

Miss Pickerell proceeded directly to the galley. When she examined it, she knew exactly what she had to do. The small electric stove most certainly needed a good scrubbing. So did the teakettle standing on one of the burners and also the yellowing sink in which several plates and cups, all cracked, rested on a discolored rubber mat.

"The Mayor hasn't gotten around to fixing everything up yet," she commented to Assistant Sheriff Swiftlee. "If I weren't so tired, I'd do something to help him right now. Tomorrow, though . . ."

She sat down on the reclining chair farthest away from the Governor. His snoring was becoming louder by the minute.

"And tomorrow," she continued, talking now to Ellie, who, she saw, was eating a few more of the sunflower seeds, "tomorrow, we'll go on with the search for your home."

She barely listened when Assistant Sheriff Swiftlee told her that she had called off the rescue squad because they no longer seemed to need it, or when Euphus showed her some of his maps and complained that he couldn't find the nearby mountains mentioned on any one of them. Her mind was still full of the droning sound she had heard. Was it something she might have read about somewhere? Or was it a sound she had actually heard before?

It was all very irritating. She tried to push the nagging memory out of her head and to concentrate on other things. She thought about the shine she would put on the Mayor's teakettle, if only she could find some cleansing powder in his galley. And she thought about the canyon that Euphus had explained and just where she might look there for Ellie's home. But the droning sound was still in her head. She was still hearing it, over and over again, when she finally fell asleep.

10
"THAT IS AGAINST THE LAW!"

"Ridiculous!" Miss Pickerell whispered in the middle of the night, when the answer to what had been rattling around in her head suddenly came to her. "It was nothing but a chain saw making that droning sound, the electric kind with those powerful teeth set in that endless chain. And I remember exactly when and where I heard it last."

She briefly reviewed in her mind the television program about science and technology that she had watched with Euphus one rainy afternoon. A very dignified, white-bearded gentleman talked in a deep voice about undeveloped countries and how they could profit by some of the uses of technology. He showed pictures of several machines and demonstrated how they worked. When he got to the chain saw, he turned on the power and the dreadful droning sound began. Euphus, Miss Pickerell recalled, said it reminded him of a dentist's drill.

"Except that this one is even worse," he said as he pressed the button to turn off the television set and decided to go outside because the rain had slowed down to a drizzle.

"MUCH worse!" Miss Pickerell commented to Ellie, who had crawled out of the knitting bag and now lay stretched across one of her feet. "And listening to it in that mountain stillness didn't make it any better. I practically felt the blood turning to ice in my veins for a second."

She firmly resolved to steel herself against any such future feelings and NOT to think of the chain saw anymore. She was able to fall asleep very easily after she had made up her mind about this.

It was in the morning, after she had succeeded in feeding Ellie a whole handful of sunflower seeds and was standing in the Mayor's galley, a cup of tea in one hand and a scouring pad in the other, that she realized the impossibility of her decision. The sound had started all over again. The Governor— sitting on a chair in the pale sunshine and trying to smooth out some of the creases in the hat he kept adjusting on his head—was asking the Assistant Sheriff, who sat next to him, about it. Mr. Gilhuly, standing with Euphus near the engine, turned around to tell him he had heard the same sound yesterday. Euphus, though nobody asked him, began to talk about the chain saw displayed on the television program.

The Governor stepped off the launch to hear the sound more distinctly. He called for Miss Pickerell after the very first steps that he took.

"Come!" he shouted. "Come and see this still most extraordinary phenomenon and bring those bird-watching glasses with you, Miss Pickerell."

He grabbed the glasses that she held out to him. He was almost choking with excitement when he announced what he saw.

"On that mountain!" he shouted. "On that steep mountain on the far side of the stream! I . . . I believe I see a helicopter there. My eyes may be deceiving me. In this remote part of the world, seemingly never before intruded upon by humans, I . . ."

Miss Pickerell grabbed the glasses back.

"Definitely a helicopter!" she said. "A helicopter with heavy chains dangling from it! And the chains are lifting a load of trees!"

She handed the glasses to Assistant Sheriff Swiftlee, who was standing next to her and impatiently waiting for them.

"The helicopter is clearing the mountain," the Assistant Sheriff reported. "It is beginning to dip. It is dipping and disappearing up the river. It . . ."

A heavy crash broke into what she was saying. Her right hand moved automatically to the gun holster attached to the belt at her hip. With her left hand she signaled for silence as she began cautiously exploring where on the mountainside a culprit might be hiding. Miss Pickerell froze.

"If only Sampson were here," she thought to herself. "His barking would drive anyone away. Or even Pumpkins—who doesn't bark, of course—would be helpful. He always stares hard at a noise that he hears and stops only when he's sure that I know about it."

But neither Sampson nor Pumpkins was here. Without them, there was only the Assistant Sheriff and the point of a gun. Miss Pickerell could hardly bear it.

She felt very relieved when Assistant Sheriff Swiftlee returned to say she could discover no one. The Assistant Sheriff, too, seemed to be breathing more freely. She was putting her gun back in the holster and was about to sit down, when the Governor called out again.

"Look!" he shouted, pointing straight ahead. "Look at that!"

The trunk of a tree was floating down the river. Euphus and Mr. Gilhuly were in the water before Miss Pickerell finished her gasp. Euphus was pushing and Mr. Gilhuly was pulling the tree trunk. Between them, they were able to get it up on the shore. Miss Pickerell hurried to examine it.

"It's from a freshly cut pine tree," she said half-aloud. "I can smell the resin. And . . . and it's like the one Ellie came floating down on. I didn't see it, but the pictures in the paper were very detailed."

"They were indeed!" the Governor, standing near her, commented.

Miss Pickerell took her time about saying anything more. When she spoke again, it was only to murmur "Forevermore!" while she slowly opened her knitting bag and took a long, very thoughtful look at Ellie.

The Governor, too, seemed to be lost in thought. His brow was furrowed, his eyes lowered, and when he finally spoke, his voice sounded as though it came out from under his eyebrows.

"If I am correct in my reasoning," he said, "that chain saw is cutting down the trees on the mountaintop and that helicopter is carrying them down for someone to cart away. And THAT is AGAINST the law."

Assistant Sheriff Swiftlee's right hand seemed to be edging toward the gun holster again.

"I have signed bills to preserve all the forests in this region," the Governor continued. "The bills are now the laws of our great State. They are laws to be carried out. I will not stand idly by while this destruction and deforestation take place."

He paused for an instant to gaze around him.

"We will hunt for those criminals who are carting the trees away," he went on. "We will walk the length of this part of the river to find them."

"Walk through that thick underbrush along the river?" Mr. Gilhuly, scratching his head in bewilderment, inquired. "It's . . . it's impossible!"

Assistant Sheriff Swiftlee threw him a long, quiet look.

"In the interests of the law," she said, "we like to believe that nothing is impossible."

She and the Governor led the march. Miss Pickerell, with Ellie in her knitting bag over one arm and the big, black umbrella hanging over the other, walked directly behind them. Euphus and Mr. Gilhuly proceeded in a more zigzag fashion.

It was a slow and unsteady walk. The ground was very uneven. In some places it seemed to sink— and once, Miss Pickerell felt herself sliding into cold wet mud. In other places the land rose with equal unexpectedness. And the outline of the river kept changing, swelling here, shrinking there, its waters a torrent of mountain white foam at one point and only a steady rippling stream at another.

The gradually deepening canyon was even more disturbing. Its towering presence, the over-awing silence, left everyone except Euphus still. He chattered on and on.

"The river cuts through the mountains here and produces a canyon," he was saying. "And a mountain can become an isolated mass of rock, completely separated from neighboring mountain ranges. I STILL can't seem to find this place on any of my maps, though."

Miss Pickerell did not always understand Euphus's scientific explanations. Sometimes, she said "I see" when she was not completely sure that she did. But what he was saying now seemed quite clear. A plan was beginning to take shape in her head. She barely noticed when Euphus darted in front of her and began running, with Mr. Gilhuly trying to catch up to him. She and the Governor and the Assistant Sheriff ran, too, when they saw a truck standing on an unpaved mountain road and the sawed trees from the helicopter being dumped into the truck. But the truck had lumbered off by the time they got there. And the helicopter had risen to perch once more on the mountaintop.

Miss Pickerell was panting so hard she could hardly find her voice. But she knew how important it was for her to bring up what she had in mind.

"We HAVE to get to the top of that mountain," she said, as calmly as she could. "The river at this point is very narrow and there are rocks we can step on to help us cross. We will ford this river to get to the mountain on the other side. Then we will walk around the base of the mountain to find a path to the top."

The Governor hesitated for only an instant.

"If we CARE about this wilderness," he replied, "we will do just that. Yes, you and I will proceed."

He did not look very happy, with his battered top hat still on his head and his waxed moustache now all stringy, as he jumped from rock to rock in the river. And he breathed very heavily when he began walking around the base of the mountain.

"My wife says I should get more exercise," he commented to Miss Pickerell. "She says I am becoming altogether too fat and flabby."

Privately, Miss Pickerell felt that it was the

Governor's wife who really needed the exercise. When she arrived with the Governor at the State Fair a few weeks ago, she was wearing a skirt that was much too tight for her. And the white pearl buttons on her silk blouse looked as though they would pop open at any moment. But Miss Pickerell did not want to argue with the Governor. Besides, she was too busy searching for a way to get up to the top of the mountain. She was also considering and reconsidering the plan she had in her head.

It was easier walking around the mountain, because there were no bushes. They trudged on and on, the Governor stopping every little while to find his next breath or to mutter to Miss Pickerell that the newspapers and the television people would be MOST interested in what he was doing. Miss Pickerell replied only that she knew what he meant. She was giving her full attention to the towering mountain. Except for some tiny green plants growing in a crevice, it was a sheer wall of rock without any break. Nowhere, absolutely nowhere, did she see even a hint of a route they might possibly take.

They gave up the search when they reached the place from which they had started. The Governor's mouth was twitching nervously. Euphus, Mr. Gilhuly, and the Assistant Sheriff were still standing on the other side of the river. The Assistant Sheriff was rubbing her eyes. Euphus and Mr. Gilhuly were looking all around them. Miss Pickerell looked up with them when the grinding hum of the helicopter sounded again.

"I'm going after that truck," Euphus shouted, racing off. "This time, I'll get it just in the nick of time."

The Assistant Sheriff and Mr. Gilhuly raced with him. The Governor waited politely for Miss Pickerell. But she shook her head.

"I've had enough exercise today," she told him, keeping her eyes down and hoping that he could not tell by the tone of her voice that this was not really why she didn't want to ford the river and chase after the truck. "I'll just wait here until you return."

"It may take a while," the Governor said anxiously.

"I'll be all right," Miss Pickerell assured him. "I'll be *right here* waiting for you to come back."

11
MISS PICKERELL CLIMBS THE IMPOSSIBLE MOUNTAIN

Miss Pickerell had no intention of waiting. What she was planning to do was to get to the top of that mountain SOMEHOW. Everything that Euphus had said led her to believe that she might well find Ellie's home at the top. The forest was up there, the forest that the pine trees were coming from. Euphus had tested Ellie and determined that she was a forest mouse. And the deep canyon that went all around the mountain could definitely be the BARRIER that he kept looking for.

"Yes," she said to Ellie as she peeked into the knitting bag. "The mountain is certainly an isolated mass of rock. Animals living up there would have to survive in isolation. That torrential river flowing in the canyon at the bottom is no help, either. I can't imagine how you were able to float down it on your tree trunk. Or for that matter, WHY."

She opened the knitting bag a little wider to get a better glimpse of the mouse. Ellie was sitting up. She looked wistfully into Miss Pickerell's eyes and let out a small, piteous sound.

"I know! I know!" Miss Pickerell told her. "You are asking me to help you. And I will! I will! I WILL get to the top of that mountain."

How she was going to do it, she still had no idea. And it might well be what Mr. Kettelson often called a fool's errand. Euphus's theories about how canyons were produced by erosion and about how animals isolated in these canyons developed differently were undoubtedly correct. Neither Professor Humwhistel nor Dr. Haggerty had disputed them. The theories would certainly account for Ellie's different appearance, especially her very long, furry ears. She would need them to protect her from the winds and the cold on that isolated mountaintop.

The thought kept flitting in and out of Miss Pickerell's head. She felt REASONABLY sure that this rocky mountaintop was where she would find Ellie's home. She could not be COMPLETELY certain, however. The perilous climb she was contemplating might indeed be for nothing.

"But I love Ellie," she said out loud. "And if I love her, I must take the chance."

She hesitated for only an instant longer. It was to think of how sorry she felt about having deceived the Governor.

"I had no choice," she added. "He would

never have let me go. He'll understand when I explain it to him."

She proceeded quickly to another inspection of the mountain. Mrs. Broadribb's bird-watching glasses, when she turned the focusing knob, gave her a very enlarged view. It seemed to her that the plants and crevices she had observed from the bottom *might* extend up the side of the mountain. And they *did* reveal some cracks and ledges up a little way from the base. She wondered whether she might possibly use them as steps in her climb. She couldn't be sure. The shifting light of the sun and the shadows it created distorted her vision and kept changing the exact position of some of the ledges and indentations. And, of course, she didn't know whether there would be any of these the farther up she went on that almost vertical wall. Mrs. Broadribb's glasses gave only a hint of some small cracks higher up. They might even be too shallow for her to set her feet into.

"I must think! I must think!" she told herself.

But even as she said this she realized it was a waste of time. And time was of the essence. There was no telling when the Governor would come back to look for her. She cast her doubts aside, rearranged her knitting bag so that it hung, with its handles securely looped, like a knapsack down her back, and resolutely straightened her hat. Then, without as much as a backward glance, she began her climb up the mountain.

The first long step that she took brought her

up to a narrow opening that she could put her foot into. The umbrella she leaned on helped her to keep her balance. She was able to take hold of a ledge a little higher up and to pull herself up this time. There were still other ledges ahead. Miss Pickerell went from one to another, her feet clinging to the ledge she was moving up from while she grabbed the one she was crawling toward. Her hands were raw from the cold. Her fingernails were broken. Her breath came in short throaty gasps that felt like convulsive sobs.

"I must go on," she told herself when she stood up for a moment from her crawling position. "And I mustn't panic. I simply must NOT panic."

But her heart stood absolutely still when she saw that there were no more ledges. There were only cracks of varying sizes, and the first of these was too far away for anything but a leap.

"I'll . . . I'll have to risk it," she told herself. "And I can't close my eyes the way I do on a ladder. This time I have to *see* where I'm going."

She pushed her eyeglasses more firmly up on her nose and gripped her umbrella again. By hooking the handle on to the crack, she was able to hoist herself up to the foothold she needed. But she was completely out of breath when she got there. She was also feeling dizzy. And the wind was blowing so gustily, she thought it might push her off the mountain at any moment. She leaned hard on her umbrella and inhaled deeply. Someone, she couldn't remember who, had told her this helped to drive the dizziness away.

But her head was reeling when she took the next step and the next and the next. She had to pause between each one to steady herself and to wait until she could gather the strength for another. She no longer looked to see how much farther she needed to go. She simply moved on and on like an automaton. Her head was spinning like a top when she reached a place that seemed to be level. She did the only thing she was still capable of. She flung herself down on the ground.

12
A LOST WORLD

When Miss Pickerell opened her eyes she had no idea where she was. For several minutes she speculated about whether she might not have wandered into a fairy tale, the kind she used to read to Rosemary when she was a very little girl. Surely, this was a world of enchantment she was part of now. The bed of pine needles she lay on was soft, and the fragrance of the pine filled the air. The trees from which the needles had fallen were taller and thicker than any she had ever imagined. The sky was barely visible through their density. And the trees themselves seemed to go on forever. It was as though no other world existed beyond their magic boundaries. This place could indeed be some sort of fairyland!

But even Rosemary didn't believe much in fairy

tales anymore. As for herself, no matter how many times she turned the idea around in her mind, Miss Pickerell couldn't figure out what she would be doing in such a story.

The mystery didn't stop there. Miss Pickerell had forgotten to wind her watch. She did not know how long she had been lying on her back under the pine tree. She couldn't recall, either, how she had gotten there. Not even the aching of her bones, or the way every muscle in her body practically screamed out in pain when she tried to move, helped her to remember. She closed her eyes again.

It was little Ellie who brought everything back to her. The mouse had come out of the knitting bag and had climbed up to rest her head on Miss Pickerell's cheek. When Miss Pickerell looked at her, she knew why she was here. And when she saw that the mouse's eyes were moist, she had to blink back her own tears.

"Is this your good-bye?" she asked. "Is this the home to which you are returning? But don't be sad. As long as I remember you, and that will be always, it will not really be good-bye."

When she finally managed to stand up, Miss Pickerell told herself that she was being a little silly.

"Animals cry out in pain just as humans do," she commented. "But as far as I know, they don't shed any tears. Dr. Haggerty said that the tears Pumpkins had in his eyes once had nothing to do with sadness. They were there because the tear ducts that wash out the eyes weren't functioning the way they were supposed to. And, as for you, Ellie, you don't even know for sure that this is your home and neither do I. We'll just walk around and see if we can find out."

They were certainly in a forest, Miss Pickerell saw when she began to walk, a mountaintop forest overlooking the ever-changing river below. And, as far as the eye could detect, there was only the vastness of space on either side. The neighboring mountains were seemingly inseparable from each other. This one stood alone, an entity complete unto itself, almost a fantasy reaching up toward the sky. No one, without making the climb to the top, would have known about the forest. A plane flying over it, if one ever did, would be going too fast to observe it very carefully. And without some idea of what *might* be up at the top, explorers could well have thought it unnecessary for them to journey to this isolated place.

"It's . . . an unknown world," Miss Pickerell whispered in awe! "A LOST world, a world lost to all but itself in this fairy-tale wilderness."

With Ellie again in her knitting bag, Miss Pickerell walked on. The forest was unlike any she had ever seen. She stared at the giant mushrooms that looked as if someone had painted them. They were red and yellow and green, not at all like the ones displayed in their little straw baskets at the Square Toe City Supermarket.

"And at such impossible prices!" Miss Pickerell muttered. "I don't know a soul who buys them."

She stared even harder when some of the mushrooms seemed to jump. But it turned out to be frogs hidden among them that were doing the jumping. They had large red and yellow and green spots.

"It's nature that painted them the exact same color as the mushrooms," Miss Pickerell said, smiling. "It's a disguise for their protection."

The caterpillar sitting on top of a green mushroom, peacefully eating its way along the plant, had another disguise. He looked like a cactus growing there. Stranger still, Miss Pickerell thought, were the two lizards, with their long bodies and tapering tails, who sat perched on a nearby rock. They looked like miniature dinosaurs.

What she found most fascinating, however, was the small snake resting on an old log. She had seen pictures of this kind of snake in a nature magazine that Professor Humwhistel had once given her. The writer in the magazine had said that the species was extinct. There were only fossil remains to identify it.

"But it's not really extinct!" Miss Pickerell exclaimed, speaking to herself and to Ellie. "It is still alive because it's safe here, safe from the dangers that nearly made it extinct. This is a wonderful unknown world I have found, a lost world hidden by the overpowering canyon."

Ellie's only answer was a sudden excited trill

and a struggle to leap out of the knitting bag. Miss Pickerell let her go. She followed her as she raced toward trees that seemed to be alive with elephant-eared mice. Some were climbing up the tree trunks. Some were nibbling busily at the seeds on the dry pine cones. Ellie sat on a rock, looking wistfully up at them. They paid no attention to her. Miss Pickerell could hardly bear the suspense. It was very possible that the mice would view her Ellie as a stranger, a stranger that they did not want in their midst.

"Poor Ellie!" Miss Pickerell breathed. "Poor little, lonely Ellie!"

Then the wonderful part began. One at a time, the mice, their ears outstretched, came gliding down from the trees to the forest floor. One at a time, they sniffed Ellie cautiously. Ellie sniffed each one in turn. And suddenly, in what seemed like an outburst of recognition and celebration, they formed a circle around her and danced and trilled with delight. They paused only to bring her some of their recently collected pine seeds as a welcome home present. And after she had eaten her fill, they drew her into the joyous dancing circle with them. Ellie was home at last!!

Miss Pickerell walked away as fast as she could. She had to, if she was not to burst out crying then and there. But she couldn't resist turning around for a last look. Ellie, no longer dancing, was doing the same. Miss Pickerell blew her a kiss.

"Be happy, Ellie," she whispered. "You are back in this beautiful lost world where you belong. I . . . I can only be happy for you."

It was at just this moment that Miss Pickerell heard the droning of the chain saw in her startled ears.

13

MR. FEE,
MR. FI, MR. FO,
AND MR. FUM

Miss Pickerell was furious. She was NOT about to let ANYONE proceed to destroy this magical world she had found.

"Never!" she said to herself. "Absolutely never!"

She thought of all the innocent creatures to whom the forest was home. They depended on it for their very survival. She HAD to make sure that they remained safe and happy there.

The chain saw was nowhere in sight. The droning was not very loud, either. Miss Pickerell meant to track down its whereabouts, though, and as fast as she could!

"Yoo hoo!" she called. "Yoo hoo!"

But the words simply resounded in the air. No one had heard her.

She kept walking in the direction from which the droning seemed to come. It was getting louder and louder and more distinct. Once, she stopped to call out a warning.

"Stop that!" she screamed. "Stop that sawing right now!"

Again, it was only her own voice that came back to her. She kept on walking.

It was almost at the edge of the forest that she saw them, the two men chain-sawing down the trees, which practically fell into the basket of the helicopter that was positioned in front of the trees. Miss Pickerell felt certain that the men must have heard the crunch of her approaching footsteps on the stony ground. But they made no move to show it.

"Stop that!" she called out again, waving her big, black umbrella in her excitement. "Stop that sawing this minute."

Both men stared. The one with the bald head and the muscles that bulged like iron bands through his shirt-sleeves said nothing. He went right on sawing. The second man put his chain saw down and walked over to her. Miss Pickerell started to shiver the instant she took a good look at his face.

"It's the witch!" she whispered. "The witch from my nightmares!"

The face she saw was long and narrow, with sunken eyes and a chin jutting out so far that it came close to touching the pointed nose above it.

Greasy black hair hung down in strings on the yellow skeletonlike cheeks. Miss Pickerell kept telling herself that, of course, this wasn't the same witch. That was nonsense! But she did consider the remote possibility that her nightmare witch might have been transformed into a man and transported to this mountaintop to stand staring menacingly at her. She was still thinking about it when the man started to talk.

"Mind your own business," he said, spitting the words out in her face. "Mind your own business and get out of here!"

"This IS my business," Miss Pickerell retorted heatedly. "It is the business of every good citizen of this country or anywhere else in the world. I'm sure you know that our own Governor has signed bills to *preserve* the forests in our State."

The man was not even listening.

"Lady," he said, "I don't know who you are and . . ."

"I'm Miss Pickerell of Square Toe Farm," Miss Pickerell said promptly.

The man let out a sneering laugh.

"And I'm Mr. Fee," he said. "My partner over there is Mr. Fi. The helicopter up front is Mr. Fo. And the robot sitting in the helicopter is Mr. Fum."

"I don't care what you call yourselves," Miss Pickerell began. "I am here to tell you . . ."

"And I don't care about what you want to tell me," the man interrupted. "You and your kind have frightened some lumbermen away. But not us, lady. And you won't convince us with your highfalutin arguments, either."

"Highfalutin . . . ?" Miss Pickerell questioned.

"That's what I said," he went on. "Maybe that works with lumbermen doing this job for a living, whether they like it or not. But me and my partner like this business we started. And we're going to keep right on sawing down these trees. As soon as we have enough on the helicopter, Mr. Fo will go down to dump them into the truck and come up again for more. Our helicopter is a very busy little chopper. We control Mr. Fum, the robot inside, by radio. The equipment is right in this box by my side. We never even had to bother learning about manual flying. Understand, lady?"

"I know all about radio-controlled planes," Miss Pickerell retorted. "My middle nephew, Euphus, has a miniature model. So have some of his friends. They're always busy flying them. In the school yard or the field near the school, I forget which . . ."

"So you have a middle nephew called Euphus!" the man said mockingly. "And he flies his miniature radio-controlled plane above a field near his school! Just think of that!!"

Miss Pickerell quickly changed the subject.

"I know about how your helicopter goes up and down, too," she said. "And about the truck that carts the trees away."

The man gave her a quick, sharp look.

"How did you get up here, anyway?" he wanted to know.

Miss Pickerell was certainly not about to tell him.

"I should think you'd be ashamed of yourselves," she said. "Both of you! Chain-sawing down these trees that are our wildlife heritage. At this rate, they'll all be gone in less than two years. The small plants, too. And the animals living in the forest who . . ."

The bald-headed man, who had so far not said a word, suddenly roared with laughter.

"She must be thinking of that curious mouse that came to see what we were doing," he said to his partner. "Remember how we tried to catch her so that we could sell her to a circus or throw her down into the river or whatever else we could think of? She went down on that tree trunk she clung to, instead, the tree trunk that . . ."

"You are a vicious, rotten man," Miss Pickerell shouted. "And I . . ."

"And I," the man standing near her interrupted, "I am telling you that we don't want you up here. I don't know how you got up here, but whatever way it was, you'd better get down the same way."

"I'm not going!" Miss Pickerell said, waving her umbrella again, right in his face this time. "What you are doing is against the law. It's . . ."

"So," the man broke in, talking very slowly, "so you're going to tip off the police, are you? Is that what you have in mind, lady?"

"What I have in mind," the bald-headed man added, "is that if she won't go by herself, we'll have to get rid of her some other way. We could dump HER in the river. That would get rid of her for good. And of her blabbing to the police, too."

The witchlike man seemed to be thinking about this.

"They wouldn't find her for a month, at least," he said, scratching his long chin. "And they wouldn't know where she came from. They wouldn't even know who she was, except for that hat, maybe, and that knitting bag. We could destroy those."

"That's . . . that's murder," Miss Pickerell said, staring aghast as she felt her heart pounding and her knees beginning to buckle under her. "You wouldn't dare."

"Maybe not," the man, also staring, replied. "But I can pummel you so hard you'll never talk again. You'll . . ."

He lunged forward, his fists beating wildly, his hands gripping her throat. Miss Pickerell, her head thrust back, was choking. She opened her mouth for a desperate breath of air and, without even knowing exactly what she was doing, leaned down and bit the hand at her throat. She bit and bit and bit. The man, screaming out in pain, reeled way back. But only for an instant. His eyes fixed solely on her, he took a step forward, then another. One more, and he would be at her again! Almost instinctively, just when he was lifting a foot to take the step, Miss Pickerell pushed the umbrella in his way. He stumbled, tried to right himself, stumbled again and fell, face down on a hard rock. The blood came pouring out of his mouth immediately. And he shouted that he had lost his two front teeth.

Miss Pickerell, draping the umbrella over her arm again, felt a surge of relief flow over her. She had not shrunk back in fear the way she did in her nightmares. Never again, if the horrible witch came back, would she be afraid of her.

But the battle was not over. The bald-headed man had now put down his chain saw. He did not speak. He simply took one slow step after another as he walked toward her. Miss Pickerell felt only a paralyzing terror. Against those bulging muscles and the burning hatred in his eyes, she had no defense. She looked about her, half moaning, half sobbing.

Then she heard the whirr of the helicopter. What the man had called his busy little chopper was responding to the programmed radio message. Its folded chains were straightening themselves out and the helicopter, with its load of freshly cut trees, was beginning to rise.

"It's my only way out," Miss Pickerell murmured desperately. "I have no choice."

She caught hold of a large, thick branch extending from one of the tree trunks a second before the bald-headed man reached her. He could do nothing when she was flung into the sky with the load. Mr. Fum, carrying out the radio-controlled order he had already been given, was off. The helicopter was descending into the canyon. And she, Miss Pickerell knew, was heading for disaster!

14
WHIRLING DOWN THE CANYON

She knew exactly what was going to happen to her. The helicopter was already whirling her down the canyon. Her pilot was a robot, a creature of computers and batteries. He could neither hear her nor rescue her. He could respond only to the radio commands of Mr. Fee and Mr. Fi on the mountaintop. And no word of mercy would come from them! She was HELPLESS, like an animal left to die in a trap.

It would be even worse when the helicopter reached its destination. The dumping into the waiting truck was automatic. She had observed that much when she watched how a previous load was emptied into the truck. Holding on to a branch near the bottom of the load, she might well be the first to go. The enormous weight of the trees that followed would fall right on her back. They would crush the life out of her.

She remembered, too, how quickly the transfer of the trees from the helicopter to the truck was completed. The man in the truck, sitting in the driver's seat, ready to speed away, would not be likely to hear her screams. In any case, she doubted that she would be able to scream. The thrashing of the wind and the helicopter's blades was tearing at her clothes, knocking the breath out of her.

"There must be something I can do about this," she told herself. "SOMETHING! Even an animal in a trap doesn't altogether give up."

But there was nothing, absolutely nothing. The helicopter was traveling rather slowly. It probably had to with such a heavy load. The progress was steady, though. They were already almost halfway down to the bottom. She buried her face against the tree branch she was clutching.

"Another of what Deputy Administrator Blakely calls my dangerous adventures!" she said tonelessly.

She could practically see him wagging his warning finger at her. Not that the Deputy Administrator ever made such an undignified gesture. But he always looked as though he wanted to. And she half-expected that he would someday.

"Whatever am I thinking of?" she suddenly exclaimed out loud. "There isn't going to be another *someday* for him to warn me again."

She opened her eyes to dare another look down the canyon. They had passed the halfway mark now. And they were still proceeding steadily.

"But the Deputy Administrator had no right to say I was getting involved in another dangerous adventure," she protested. "I didn't know that I was going to meet Mr. Fee and Mr. Fi. All I was doing was looking for Ellie's home. Somebody HAD to do that!"

Ellie, Miss Pickerell reflected, had probably taken the exact same route on this exact same helicopter. She, too, had escaped to a tree to get away from those villainous men on the mountain. And her tree had also ended up on the helicopter bound for the truck.

"Only her tree trunk must have fallen off the helicopter," Miss Pickerell reasoned. "And it fell down into the river. Dear little Ellie! At least I was able to do something for her."

The thought gave Miss Pickerell some comfort. She smiled when she remembered Ellie dancing happily and trilling with her friends.

She stopped smiling when she glanced down the canyon again. They had traveled another considerable distance. Soon, soon . . .

The wind was rising still more. The air smelled damp and cold. Miss Pickerell felt herself shivering in every part of her body. Her mouth trembled, her teeth chattered, her eyes blinked uncontrollably. And her heart, which seemed to have grown to an enormous size, was beating like a drum against her ribs.

"I must stop this," she told herself firmly. "I must be brave about what is coming."

She took a last long look at the tops of the trees she was approaching and at the shining river below them. Then she slowly closed her eyes and waited.

15
THE RESCUE
IN THE SKY

Miss Pickerell did not have long to wait. She had
just about finished shutting her eyes when the helicopter began to change its course. She could feel
the way it was veering up the river. And it was also
very definitely picking up speed.

"This must be the final maneuver," Miss
Pickerell said to herself hoarsely. "Mr. Fum, the
robot, is steering directly toward the truck now.
I'm sure of it. I remember precisely where the truck
was standing."

But she could not at all understand why the
speed should be accelerated at this point. It seemed
to her that a slowdown would be more appropriate
before a landing. And she simply could not figure
out what the distant grinding hum that she heard
at this moment could possibly be.

"It sounds like a very angry wasp," she said thoughtfully. "But that's ridiculous, of course."

The sound grew more distinct as it came closer. It was beginning to resemble the drone of a helicopter.

"Mr. Fee and Mr. Fi couldn't really have two helicopters," Miss Pickerell reasoned. "They would surely have wanted to brag about it and to have mentioned it to me."

She could not resist the temptation to open her eyes and to look around. The sky was blue and empty of anything but some fleecy white clouds. Nowhere was there a sign of an angry wasp or of another helicopter.

"My imagination is playing tricks on me," she decided sadly. "That sometimes happens to people in moments of crisis, I know. I'd better make sure."

With the hand that was not clutching the tree branch, she managed to reach for Mrs. Broadribb's bird-watching glasses. She peered through them in every direction. Still nothing! She was just about to lower the glasses when she saw the second helicopter. It was rattling into sight over the tops of the trees near the river. And it didn't look anything like the helicopter she was on. It was much bigger and it was painted a bright red and blue.

"The Square Toe City helicopter!" she whispered. "The one that the Mayor bought last year."

And now she knew why Mr. Fum was driving so fast. He was acting on radio instructions from the mountaintop. Mr. Fee and Mr. Fi must have seen the Mayor's helicopter approach long before she did. Mr. Fum was trying frantically to unload the trees into the truck before the red and blue helicopter caught up with him.

"He'll probably succeed, too," Miss Pickerell moaned, holding on tight to her branch, while the helicopter lurched forward at an incredible speed. "We haven't very far to go now. The Mayor has come too late."

She could hear someone on the Mayor's helicopter shouting through a bullhorn. It was a man ordering Mr. Fum not to drop the load into the truck. Another voice, this one higher and more like a woman's, took the bullhorn to plead for Miss Pickerell's life. Mr. Fum kept speeding on. The first voice came back on the bullhorn.

"We're going to confiscate your helicopter, you know," the voice announced calmly.

Mr. Fum paused as if he were waiting for instructions, then turned to fly the helicopter up the river.

"He's trying to escape," Miss Pickerell whispered. "To escape with his precious chopper as fast as he can."

But escape seemed out of the question. The heavy load of trees was slowing up the flight. And the Mayor's helicopter was moving closer and closer.

Another momentary pause! Another lightning

turn! Down the canyon again! Mr. Fee and Mr. Fi had made up their minds to risk it. Mr. Fum was again flying toward the truck. The Mayor's helicopter was in pursuit. But Mr. Fum was nearing the bottom. Miss Pickerell whispered, "Forevermore!"

The Mayor had not given up, however. Miss Pickerell saw a bucket seat being lowered from the helicopter, the kind of seat with a rounded back that looks like a playground swing. And the Mayor was sitting on the very edge, his arms stretched out toward her. He was going to SNATCH her from Mr. Fee's chopper before it was too late.

But no matter how much he stretched or leaned forward, he couldn't reach her. Miss Pickerell heard the gnashing of his teeth as he tried again and again. Once, he managed to grab hold of the strings of her knitting bag. But that was all.

Miss Pickerell was not about to give up when rescue seemed so close, either. She attempted a leap when the Mayor reached for her again. He lifted her up and out the instant he got a hold on her. At the exact same moment, Mr. Fee poised his helicopter and, the engines throbbing, got ready to land.

Miss Pickerell felt herself almost sinking into unconsciousness, when the bucket seat, with her and the Mayor on it, was hoisted up into his helicopter. But she refused the smelling salts that Miss Ogelthorpe, appearing from somewhere in the back, was offering her. She was too intent on watching the robot-piloted helicopter to pay any attention to her dizziness. Mr. Fum had dumped the lumber into the river to lighten the load, she noticed, and was now flying up to the mountaintop again.

"After him! After him!" she shouted. "We must get those chain-saw criminals arrested!"

Mr. Fee and Mr. Fi had already escaped in the helicopter with Mr. Fum by the time the Mayor's helicopter got to the mountaintop. But Miss Pickerell was not discouraged.

"They've left their radio box behind!" she announced. "I can steer them off their course. We must land this instant so that I can begin!"

She knew exactly how to work the radio communication box. Euphus had given her expert instructions. The orders she issued to Mr. Fum with the instrument would land him and his companions where the Mayor told her the Assistant Sheriff and other police were waiting. The arrest would be very swift.

When Miss Pickerell returned to the helicopter she leaned comfortably back in the seat that the Mayor settled her in. She listened quietly to the lady reporter, who was telling her about how the Assistant Sheriff had radioed for help the minute she learned that Miss Pickerell had started her climb, and about how the Mayor had immediately volunteered his assistance. But she stopped listening in the middle of the story. The Mayor's pilot had turned around to say that Mr. Fee and Mr.

Fi were now flying in a direction away from the mountain road.

"They don't know anything about manual flying," Miss Pickerell said immediately. "They must have another radio box or some other radio control right there with them."

The Mayor seemed about to wring his hands. Miss Pickerell did not feel half so dismayed. In her mind, the problem almost solved itself.

"Then we will override their signals," she said.

The expression on the Mayor's face changed from despair to bewilderment.

"With that powerful radio control device you had installed on this helicopter last week," Miss Pickerell reminded him. "Mr. Kettelson heard all about it from Miss Lemon. She said it was for chasing the dope-smuggling helicopters that . . ."

"Yes, yes," the Mayor broke in. "But it's a new, experimental device. "We've never even had a chance to try it out. We . . ."

"Well, I soon will have," Miss Pickerell told him. "And if it's anything like that radio box, I'll manage."

She was next to the pilot before anyone could stop her. She watched happily as she saw how her very powerful radio signals were overriding those in the little chopper. Mr. Fee and Mr. Fi were being steered right into the mountain-road clearing. And now, they WOULD be arrested!

She walked slowly back and sank wearily into

her seat. She couldn't remember ever having been so tired before. And her dizziness was getting worse and worse. This time, when Miss Ogelthorpe offered her the smelling salts, she did not refuse.

16

"I MISS MY LITTLE ELLIE"

Nobody, but absolutely nobody, stayed away from the luncheon party the Governor gave for Miss Pickerell the very next Sunday. It was held in the banquet hall of the Governor's mansion at the State Capital. Guests from neighboring areas came by car, by bus, and by train. From farther away, they arrived by plane and by helicopter. Even the President and his wife were there for a little while. The President's wife refused to taste as much as a bite of the delicious cherry cake dessert. She needed to watch her weight, she said. The Governor's wife commented that she wished she had such self-control. She helped herself to two portions of the cake.

The speeches began after the dishes were cleared way. The President spoke first. He explained that he was still suffering from his usual springtime cold. Everybody knew about the cold. The newspapers had described all the details. But, he added, he could NOT let a little fever and a sore throat keep him from attending Miss Pickerell's party. Thunderous applause followed this remark. It also followed his statement about good intentions. Those were never enough, he said. Good intentions had to be acted upon. And that was what Miss Pickerell had done. She had risked life and limb for the sake of an endangered animal and for the survival of a part of the great American wilderness where the animal lived. He turned to Miss Pickerell, who said, "Thank you, Mr. President."

He ended his speech by saying that he hated to go but he was afraid that he really needed to get back to bed. He shook hands with Miss Pickerell before he left. Miss Pickerell cautioned him to be sure to drink plenty of liquids, especially tea with lemon. She also recommended hot chicken soup.

"It's as good as penicillin," she urged. "And much more nourishing. One needs plenty of nourishment during an illness."

The reporters and the television cameras pursued the President, the President's wife, and their two very tall Secret Service agents right up to the door at the far end of the banquet hall. The guests, in a standing ovation, clapped their hands, stamped their feet, and cheered. The Mayor, standing next to Miss Pickerell at the long table on the stage in front of the room, clapped the hardest of all.

"The President had a very ample lunch," he commented to her, when he sat down again. "I did not think much of the meal, myself. It lacked both originality and imagination."

Miss Pickerell had nothing to say about the food. She had been too busy concentrating on the way her fancy new shoes were pinching her toes to pay much attention to what she was eating.

"My oldest niece, Rosemary, persuaded me to buy them," she said to the Mayor. "I should have gotten the kind I always wear, the oxfords with the laces. Or even a pair of nice sneakers. Everybody is wearing them these days, even on television talk shows. Mrs. Broadribb, sitting near the window over there, is wearing them right now."

"What?" the Mayor asked, gasping a little. "What did you say, Miss Pickerell? About Mrs. Broadribb and the sneakers?"

Miss Pickerell had no chance to explain. The Governor was banging with his gavel and shouting into the microphone for attention.

"Ladies and gentlemen," he said, when everybody was quiet again, "His Honor, the Mayor of Square Toe City, has generously volunteered to be our first speaker, the first after the President, that is. I'm sure we all welcome him gladly."

The Mayor practically bounced over to the microphone. He smiled broadly when he began to speak.

"The President's appearance is a tough act to

follow," he said. "I have therefore decided not to make a speech at all. I will show you some slides instead. The pictures were taken on my helicopter by Miss Olga Ogelthorpe, star reporter of the *Square Toe Gazette.*"

The Governor gulped so distinctly, Miss Pickerell was afraid that everybody at the small round tables right in front of the stage, including her seven nieces and nephews and their parents, the three ladies from the Why Not Knit It Shoppe, Mr. Kettelson, the hardware store man, Mr. Esticott, the train conductor, and Assistant Sheriff Stella T. Swiftlee, could hear him. The Mayor simply smiled and continued.

"The pictures show the actual rescue of our brave Miss Pickerell from the dreadful end that was awaiting her. Are you ready, Miss Ogelthorpe?"

Miss Ogelthorpe, wearing a pink and white dress with a straw hat to match, stood behind a projector in the back of the room. The pictures she flashed on the wall above the stage were very large and in brilliant color. The first two showed Miss Pickerell clinging to the tree trunk in the helicopter that was hurling her down the canyon. The third, fourth, and fifth pictures displayed the Mayor reaching out to her while in his perilous position on the bucket seat. The sixth and final picture was the actual rescue, a vivid portrayal of the way the Mayor took hold of Miss Pickerell and lifted her up and into the bucket seat with him.

"There was no time for any more, any more

pictures, I mean," the Mayor apologized, as he and Miss Ogelthorpe bowed.

Nobody heard him. The applause was too deafening. And the chattering was almost as loud.

Most of the guests were still talking when Mr. Trilling gave his speech about how he had permitted Miss Pickerell to enter the Deputy Administrator's conference room and about how Mr. Blakely, as a kind of apology to Miss Pickerell for the unkind things he had said about the mouse, was now on her farm, keeping an eye on her animals while she was away. And some of the guests went right on talking when Miss Lemon made her speech about being the very first one in all of Square Toe County to advise Miss Pickerell of the presence of the strange animal in their midst. Miss Lemon was also wearing a pink and white dress, Miss Pickerell observed. But Miss Lemon wore flowers in her hair instead of a hat. And she had on pink and white lace gloves.

The room became completely quiet only when Professor Humwhistel rose from his seat on the podium. He waved away the television reporters who were rushing toward him.

"You will have far more important people than me to photograph in a minute," he said. "I introduce to you first a world-renowned figure who surely needs no introduction. Dr. R. R. Michaels, of the International Environmental Fund, has flown across the country to address you today. He . . ."

Professor Humwhistel could not finish his sentence. Tumultuous applause was greeting the gray-haired gentleman who came forward. He spoke very quietly about the senseless destruction of the American wilderness and, still more quietly, about the dreadful cruelty inflicted on innocent animals. And meeting Miss Pickerell was a hope and inspiration for him, he said. There were sobs in the banquet hall when he sat down. Even Assistant Sheriff Swiftlee, normally so cool and collected, was drying her eyes with a crisp white handkerchief, Miss Pickerell noticed.

Dr. Haggerty, also sitting on the podium, introduced the next speaker, Mrs. Lucy Wright, who was representing the American Wildlife Federation. She pleaded for help and understanding of the kind Miss Pickerell and the Governor had demonstrated.

"They are an example to us all," she said. "Miss Pickerell did not hesitate for a moment to embark on her errand of mercy. And your Governor, busy as he is, insisted on accompanying her. Only a very brave person would have ventured forth to encounter the dangers of that raging river. And he has informed me that he is now urging his State legislators to enact laws to preserve existing refuge areas for animals and plants, to provide still more such areas, and to protect them all adequately. Swift conviction will follow the arrest of violators. The Governor will see to that!"

The Governor came forward to a burst of roaring cheers. He stroked his moustache while he waited for the room to become quiet.

"I have never shirked the responsibility to keep our great State on the map," he said as he began his talk. "And I have taken the time to record my memoirs of this most important journey on tape. They are now in the hands of Mr. Clanghorn, the editor of the *Square Toe Gazette*, who is going to serialize them in his daily newspaper. I am inviting the Mayor to add his pictures to my articles."

The Governor beamed at the Mayor. The Mayor nodded grimly.

"And now," the Governor went on, "I have the great honor to bring to the platform a budding young scientist, already known to many of you. It was his testing that revealed Ellie as a forest mouse and his theories about where she might have come from that made it possible to find her home. Ladies and gentlemen, Miss Pickerell's middle nephew, Euphus!"

Euphus gave his speech about geographic isolation to tumultuous applause. He also posed carefully for the television cameras, standing up very straight and looking very serious. Miss Pickerell sat openmouthed, watching him. She nearly slid off her chair when she also heard him tell the reporters that he was available for a press conference. The Governor saved her just in time.

"Come, Miss Pickerell," he said, as he extended his hand and escorted her to the microphone.

"But wait!! Before you say a word, let me give you what the President has left for you."

He took a small white box out of his pocket, opened it, and held up a gleaming gold medal on a chain.

"It is the Medal of Honor from the White House," he told her. "And I will read you what the President has inscribed on it.

FOR MISS PICKERELL, WHO FOUND A LOST WORLD ON THE MOUNTAIN AND SAVED THE LIVING CREATURES THAT CALLED IT HOME."

Rosemary rushed up to help Miss Pickerell put on the chain and to center the medal so that everybody could see it. The television cameras went into immediate action. Their flashing lights nearly blinded Miss Pickerell. And she felt so choked up she could hardly talk.

"I want to thank all of you for this wonderful celebration," she said finally. "And I thank the President for the great honor he has bestowed on me. Most of all, I feel, I should thank the Mayor. He saved my life. Without his brave help, I wouldn't be here today."

"The Mayor! The Mayor!" everybody shouted.

The Mayor stood up to acknowledge the applause. Miss Pickerell was glad to see that he was smiling again. She took a deep breath and spoke into the microphone again.

"I have only a little bit more to say," she went on. "And that is to tell you that I did only what I had to do. I will always love animals and birds and flowers and the beautiful trees that grow in our land. And I will always do what I can to protect them."

She tried to get back to her seat. Her shoes were pinching more and more. But the reporters swarmed around her. They had to shout the questions they asked to make themselves heard above the uproarious din of the clapping and cheering. Mr. Clanghorn, the *Square Toe Gazette* editor, an observant man, persuaded them to leave. He brought her a chair and sat down with her.

"We are old friends," he said, "and you know that I will not print anything you say without your permission. Tell me honestly, Miss Pickerell, what are you thinking of now, at this great moment of celebration and honor?"

Miss Pickerell took a long time to answer.

"Mostly of Ellie," she said at last. "I know that she and all animals have their own lives to live. And I could not keep her where she did not belong. But . . ."

She paused to let out a very small sigh.

"But," she went on, "but I can't help myself. I miss my little Ellie."

Mr. Clanghorn, who understood, sighed with her.

ABOUT THE AUTHORS

Ellen MacGregor created the character of Miss Pickerell in the early 1950s. With a little help from Miss MacGregor, Lavinia Pickerell had four remarkable adventures. Then, in 1954, Ellen MacGregor died. And it was not until 1964, after a long, long search, that Miss P. finally found Dora Pantell.

Dora Pantell says that she has been writing something at some time practically since she was born. Among the "somethings" are scripts for radio and television, magazine stories, newspaper articles, books for all ages, and, of course, the Miss Pickerell adventures, which, she insists, she enjoys best of all. As good places for writing, she suggests airplanes, dentists' waiting rooms, and a semi-dark theater when the drama gets dull. Ms. Pantell spends a good deal of the rest of her time reading nonviolent detective stories, playing or listening to classical music, and watching the television shows on New York City's Channel 13. But mostly she is busy keeping the peace among her three cats, Haiku Darling, Cluny Brown, and the newest addition, Katy Did.

ABOUT THE ARTIST

Charles Geer has been illustrating for as long as he can remember and has more books to his credit than he can count. He lives in a rambling old house on the Chesapeake, on Maryland's Eastern Shore. When he is not bent over the drawing board or the typewriter—Mr. Geer has written as well as illustrated two middle-group books—he is out on the twenty-two-foot sailboat he built himself or taking long backpacking hikes.